Anonymous

A Review of the Relative Commercial Progress of the Cities of New York & Philadelphia

SALZWASSER
VERLAG

Anonymous

A Review of the Relative Commercial Progress of the Cities of New York & Philadelphia

Reprint of the original, first published in 1859.

1st Edition 2022 | ISBN: 978-3-37512-272-0

Verlag (Publisher): Salzwasser Verlag GmbH, Zeilweg 44, 60439 Frankfurt, Deutschland
Vertretungsberechtigt (Authorized to represent): E. Roepke, Zeilweg 44, 60439 Frankfurt, Deutschland
Druck (Print): Books on Demand GmbH, In de Tarpen 42, 22848 Norderstedt, Deutschland

A REVIEW

OF THE

RELATIVE COMMERCIAL PROGRESS

OF THE CITIES OF

New-York & Philadelphia,

TRACING THE DECLINE OF THE LATTER

TO STATE DEVELOPMENT,

AND SHOWING THE NECESSITY OF

TRANS-ATLANTIC STEAMSHIP COMMUNICATION

TO RE-ESTABLISH FOREIGN TRADE.

A REVIEW

OF THE

RELATIVE COMMERCIAL PROGRESS

OF THE CITIES OF

New-York & Philadelphia,

TRACING THE DECLINE OF THE LATTER

TO STATE DEVELOPMENT,

AND SHOWING THE NECESSITY OF

TRANS-ATLANTIC STEAMSHIP COMMUNICATION

TO RE-ESTABLISH FOREIGN TRADE.

PHILADELPHIA:

JACKSON, PRINTER.

1859.

Philadelphia, Jan. 8th, 1859.

G. W. BAKER, Esq.,

DEAR SIR,—Having been favored with a view of a Manuscript prepared by yourself, containing much valuable and interesting information upon the present Commercial Status of our City, and the means necessary for the development of our Foreign Trade, the Corn Exchange Association has instructed the undersigned Committee to solicit of you the right to publish the same. Although originally prepared for private use, we trust you will not withhold information which should be in the hands of every business man in the Community.

We have the honor to be,

Very respectfully yours,

GEO. L. BUZBY,
SAMUEL L. WITMER,
F. A. GODWIN,
HOWARD HINCHMAN,
Committee.

———————————•◆◆▸———————————

Philadelphia, Jan. 10th, 1859.

GENTLEMEN,—

I have the honor of acknowledging your favor of the 8th instant, requesting, by instruction of the Corn Exchange Association, the right to publish the Manuscript to which you have so kindly alluded.

As you observe, it was not intended for publication, having been prepared for the use of Mr. Baker, the Collector of the Port. Impressed with the conviction that some plan could be adopted to establish a line of Steam-Ships for the promotion of Commerce, he wished to bring the matter before a few of the business men of this City. This manuscript having become too elaborate for hand to hand reading, it was replaced by a brief pamphlet, which, to some extent, has already been circulated.

With the hope that this may assist in directing public attention to a matter of so great importance to the interests of Philadelphia, it is most cheerfully placed in your hands for publication, under the auspices of the Corn Exchange Association.

Permit me to acknowledge the honor you have conferred upon me, and to subscribe myself,

Your Humble and Obedient Servant,

G. W. BAKER.

GEO. L. BUZBY,
SAMUEL L. WITMER,
F. A. GODWIN,
HOWARD HINCHMAN,
} *Committee.*

Contents.

———•••———

Introduction.

By the business circles of Philadelphia, it is admitted, that a point has been reached in her history, from which further commercial progress is impossible, and from which recession is inevitable, unless her people can be stimulated to *harmonize* upon some project, which will encourage the one, in order to prevent the other. By very many this crisis has long been foreseen; and by some, efforts have been made to concentrate private enterprise, with the view of supplying those facilities indispensable in the prosecution of foreign trade. To those who have no knowledge of the business habits, proclivities and antagonisms of Philadelphians, the failure of such attempts would simply prove that they were insensible to their own interests—but a resident observer would charge it to "individualism." He would be compelled, however reluctantly, to admit, that the mercantile classes had but seldom hazarded their individual interests, by uniting them for the liberal encouragement of public enterprise, and rarely permitted themselves to look beyond the narrow circle by which their own interests were circumscribed; and, accordingly, when the circle of one comes in conflict with that of another, both feel, what neither will acknowledge, jealousy. It is quite as lamentable, as it is true, that this unacknowledged sentiment, so hostile to public enterprise, forms the strata from which so many diversified veins of opinion out-crop, which separately produce no profit, and cannot be advantageously united.

But it would be an unpleasant, as well as an unprofitable task, to call attention to those idiosyncracies of unchecked impulse, which divide the business community, and antagonize the different classes, so as to prevent that intermingling of individuals which would consolidate them into one friendly association. These defects, if we may so call them, can only be remedied

1

by sinking self for the public good, by the promotion of which, individual good is always most rapidly advanced. We may say, in passing, that this is not peculiar to the business community: the learned professions feel the absence of that generous liberality of intercourse, which is not only an essential to brotherhood, but required for the encouragement of enterprise in intellect, so often depressed through the fear of that detraction, by which mediocrity strives to keep all upon a common platform.

We do not, however, feel the same delicacy in speaking of that *conservatism* which is an attribute, and to some extent, unquestionably, a political virtue, in the character of all Pennsylvanians. Its characteristic is imperturbability. It is often so slow of conviction, that it seldom takes the tide "at the flood." It deliberates until the opportunity is lost; but when the oversight grows into irremedial wrong, even prudence is abandoned in the hot haste for an impossible remedy. But this is generalizing. Let us illustrate by some specialities which will show how the people of the City and the State have fallen behind from the prevalence of this conservatism in business, this " masterly inactivity" which quietly permits the rest of mankind to overreach Pennsylvanians.

We will first instance a very recent case which has occasioned much tribulation and excitement in certain quarters. The Kensington and Baltimore Depots were united by one of the City Passenger Railroads. By this means, through passengers could pass from one depot to the other, without being compelled to hire a carriage, ride in an omnibus, or *stay-over* in our City. Conservatism took the alarm, and in lieu of that action which would have anticipated and prevented the real evil, an indiscriminate attack was made upon corporate monopolies : those associations of private capital and enterprise, which give labor to the poor, bring ease to the wealthy, and become the adjuncts, as they are the exponents, of the progress of society. It preferred the old institutions, the carriage and the bus, to the passenger cars—and instead of placing an embargo upon the departure of *the trains*, it would place it upon the transit—prevent all egress from the city after night, by denying the right of way through it. Was it not conservatism, to give it a dignified name, that prevented Philadelphians from timely and boldly controling the several roads, terminating in the city, sufficiently to prevent the *starting of trains* after a certain hour of the evening. When a system of connections is made for passengers who buy through tickets, it is too late to say to them "come tarry with us over night and pay your bill in the morning."

The management of such affairs in the anti-conservative City of New York, does not permit a train of cars to leave after a fixed hour in the evening. To the North, to the West, and to the South, there are MIDNIGHT TRAINS FROM PHILADELPHIA. If this system is an evidence of the supremacy of New York enterprise in controlling our roads, the attempt to counteract the results of it, by throwing obstacles in the way of transit from depot to depot, can only cause the application of the story of that conservative country gentleman, who would not be persuaded to lock his stable-door because " his horse had been, hitherto, unmolested," but betrayed a wonderful enterprise in procuring locks, bolts and bars, after the animal had disappeared.

May we not also term that conservatism of the contracted kind, which allows the Rail Road influence of New York, to so fix the price of through tickets to the south, via Philadelphia, that it is preferable for a citizen of Philadelphia, or any Pennsylvanian, having to come to this city to go south, to go to New York, spend one day, and *there* buy his ticket, say to Nashville, Tennessee, than for either to purchase the ticket at the office in Philadelphia? May not the same, in effect, be said of both passengers and freight carried by other roads in this Commonwealth, where a discrimination is now forced against our local interests? This results from acting too long upon that "hold-fast" principle, whilst our neighbors not only do that, but take the best out of everything upon which their enterprise fastens.

It would be a matter of gratulation, if the people of the State were not amenable to the same charge, of being too slow in recognising the claims of home enterprise, and for being too deficient in that State pride, which would otherwise have prevented foreign corporations from gaining the control of some of our internal improvements. In commencing her system,

conservatism prevailed, until New York had almost completed the Erie Canal, which gave her the absolute advantage of ten years profit in the Western trade. This was
increased to thirty, by failing to perfect the State works, and
refusing to allow private corporations to compete in this trade,
unless with illiberal restrictions. It would require but a
slight investigation to show, that many corporations have been
chartered within our State, for the purpose of transfering the
franchise to citizens of New York; and in some of these instances, the charter would not have been asked for, and, possibly, not granted, if our own people alone had been concerned
in the enterprise. The north-eastern section of our State, and
many of the counties comprising the northern tier, will, in this
way, soon have their rail-road facilities controlled for the benefit
of New York. Even Reading will soon be tapped, in order to
carry northward her iron productions and the coal which centres
there and along the routes, to the injury of Philadelphia-ward
routes and home trade. The Reading Rail Road has fallen
under the sway of English capitalists, and State pride is not
offended, but modestly bows to the dictation of foreign enterprise and capital.

When has an united voice from Pennsylvanians been heard in
the Halls of Congress, demanding that legislation which her
peculiar staples required? When has she retorted upon other
States, that they have rejected her just demands? and now she
adopts the motto, " Millions for defence, but not one cent for
tribute." When will she become dissatisfied with voting sub-
sidies to establish Mail privileges—*to assist the Commerce of
other Ports,*—with assisting to lavish public money to enrich and
adorn any other City than her own metropolis,—and yet be satisfied with the *ex gracia* donations of the dribblings from the Public
Treasury?

We might thus go on, almost ad infinitum, and among others,
cite the conservatism that clings to the antiquated system of civil
and criminal judicature, so burthened with confusion, that while
the one has become the highway of liberty to wealthy criminals,
the other has become a vexatious gill-net to the honest suitor,
spread and drawn by the dishonest. The effect of this is
to check the influx of foreign capital. But the limits of an

introduction advises us to reach the subjects intended to be treated in the body of this pamphlet. We will not, however, apologise for this digression. It was purposely done, in the hope that reflection might follow upon the reading of things in print, about which every one talks, over which all lament, but none essay to change. Should this be realized, so that thrifty action would tread quickly upon the heels of reflection, then we have done well thus to preface our subject. All would then be prepared to look upon another picture, by which we intend to show the Cornucopia of State wealth in the results of domestic enterprise; and while the State pride of every Pennsylvanian was thus being tickled, they would be forced to ask, " what *may* we now do to complete, or add to, this magnificence ?"

It is the object of this pamphlet to give an answer to their question, and it may be briefly and at once written down thus, ESTABLISH A LINE OF STEAMERS *to ply between Philadelphia and Foreign Ports.*

Previous to the commencement of the present century, Philadelphia was the chief Commercial Port of the United States. She has gradually retrograded, in this respect, to a humiliating inferiority, especially when her trade is compared with that of New York. This recession has taken place whilst the trade of almost every other important Port has been advancing. Had the domestic trade and industry of Philadelphia been subjected to the same neglect as her Commerce, she would not possess to-day one tithe of that wealth and population which gives her the rank of the Second City of the Union ; and the State, possibly, the first in the elements of actual wealth. Her early success in Commercial pursuits, however, attracted population and induced the peopling of the interior Valleys of the State, and became the the means, as well as the source, of State development. Hence, to the early Commercial prosperity of the City, the opening of the mines, the building of roads, and the digging of canals, is mainly owing; and out of these has grown that amazing progress in manufacturing, in wealth and population, which places Pennsylvania, in a domestic point of view, beyond parallel. It is not pretended that the City furnished all the capital required to accomplish this great progress; but she did furnish the nucleus, about which State and foreign capital formed only the nebula. But all this was done at the expense of Commerce. Railroads were made to penetrate where canals were impracticable or incompetent, until by the union of both, every portion of the State has been reached, and the great West brought into communication with the East. But here enterprise ceased, or was exhausted. No means were left, or the disposition was wanting, to improve seaward transportation, with that modern appliance which has revolutionized it upon land.

Steam upon the ocean must be a counterpoise to steam upon the land, or no hope need be entertained for commercial success.

In showing that steam vessels have become the *sine qua non* of foreign trade, it must unquestionably follow, that neither the City nor State do now enjoy the benefits which should flow from their vast expenditure for internal improvement. This default is, therefore, a direct injury to both. But in order to prove this, it seemed necessary to trace the decline of foreign trade at this port to that specific want—STEAM-VESSELS FOR IMPORT AND EXPORT TRADE. Erroneous impressions, too, have been entertained, implying that the inland location of Philadelphia was the cause of her commercial declension. It was essential to controvert them. This is done by reviewing her commercial history, and contrasting it with that of New York, giving the history of the latter, however, precedence to the former. By adopting that order and method, we could more readily develope the fact, that Philadelphia was now, not only placed in a condition to create a large foreign trade, but that nothing prevented her from competing with New York in the future, excepting the difference in their facilities for seaward transportation.

THE NATURAL ADVANTAGES POSSESSED BY THE STATE OF NEW YORK FOR EARLY SETTLEMENT AND COMMERCE.

No one of the original Thirteen States possessed naturalfacilities for settlement and commerce, superior to those of New York. This was especially true of the eastern portion, to the fertile and extensive vallies of which immigration was early invited, and from which the productions of the soil found easy transit to the sea. Thus, from the east, the Hoosic, and from the west, the Mohawk rivers, collected the products of their circumjacent vallies and carried them to the majestic Hudson, which, for 300 miles, ran a marginal course to the Sea, receiving and distributing the rivulets of trade, from either bank, within the State. Her excellent and capacious harbor received, and by means of the Passaic, controlled the trade of Northern Jersey, and by means of the Sound, attracted that of Southern Connecticut and Rhode Island, as well as Long Island.

These were vast primary inducements for a commercial people to settle in the City of New York, and transfer the calculating thrift and mercantile enterprise from old Amsterdam to the New. No great period of time elapsed before all their energies and means for business were called into active exertion. About the year 1795, and afterwards for nearly fifteen years, the European Wars taxed the energies of the New World for the support of the Old. By means of this profitable stimulant, the productive powers of nearly the whole Atlantic Coast were worked to their fullest capacity, and everything was forwarded to the Sea-port cities that the cost of transportation did not prohibit.

For the five years prior to 1795, the aggregate Export trade of Philadelphia exceeded that of New York, for the same period, nearly $9,000,000 ; but during the five following years, the aggregate of the latter increased over 200 per cent., whilst that of the former gained not quite 100 per cent. The aggregate from 1800 to 1805, shows that the highest point of demand had been reached ; in this period the export trade of New York increased 16.6 per cent., and that of Philadelphia less than $\frac{1}{3}$ of one per cent. over the preceding five years. In the next five, the former lost about $\frac{1}{4}$ of one per cent., and the latter about $6\frac{1}{3}$ per cent. During the first half of the next decade, the war of 1812 seriously affected the export trade of the entire country; but from 1815 to 1820, New York again increased 108.5 per cent., whilst Philadelphia added only 46 per cent. to the aggregate of the preceding period.

The population of the state of New York in 1790, was nearly 100,000 less than that of Pennsylvania; yet the census of 1800 shows the increase of the former to have been 72.5 per cent. and the latter 38.7 per cent. Hence, the smallest population made the largest increase of exports, and advanced in numbers 33.8 per cent. more rapidly. The ratio of increase of population for the next ten years was 63.4 and 34.4 respectively, giving New Yorrk in 1810 a larger population than Pennsylvania. The census of 1820 places the ratio at 43.1 and 29.5 per cent. increase.

These statistic results flow from the natural causes governing early settlements and production. Exports, indicating the amount of surplus, can only be gathered from that extent of area from which the cost of transportation, added to the cost of production, would leave a margin for profit in market. Assuming the cost of production to be equal in both States, the cost of transportation would limit the area in each from which trade would be supplied. In the very commencement of commercial enterprise, therefore, it appears that New York was fed from a greater extent of productive country, and enjoyed greater natural facilities for conveyance, than Philadelphia. The same principles might be observed in the preference given to New York by emigrants. During the thirty years, from 1790 to 1820, she gained, in this kind of population, 100 per cent. more than Pennsylvania.

Such were some of the natural advantages upon which the foreign trade of the City of New York was founded.

THE TRADE OF THE WEST SECURED TO NEW YORK BY THE "ERIE CANAL."

After the War of 1812, the movements of population extended more rapidly than formerly to the wilderness and prairies of the West. The first wave of Westward Immigration terminated in Ohio. Those which followed reached Indiana, and then widened their circles over territory, from which Illinois and Michigan speedily sprung into full grown States. This Western growth very soon arrested public attention in the East. There was no natural outlet or communication with tide water for that vast region, except by means of the Ohio and the Mississippi. The distance opposed insuperable objections to the use of this route, so that the tempting prize awaited the enterprise of the East. The States of Virginia and Pennsylvania each, early in their history, *thought* of connecting in the one case, the Delaware, and in the other, the Chesapeake, by canal with the west. The magnitude of such an undertaking intimidated, for a while, both individual and State enterprise, and the general government was thought to be the only source from which sufficient means could be furnished.

The failure to obtain national aid, still left the matter open to the competition of the three Atlantic States, through one of which the line of communication must find a practicable location. Three considerations placed the undertaking within the capacity of New York; namely, capital, enterprise and route. The two former, the result of her already large success in trade, and the latter, a topographical advantage, which made it possible and easy to reach the Lakes, by a line running North of those mountain ridges which interposed serious obstacles further South. The genius and public spirit of her people siezed upon the scheme, and Legislative action matured the plan and provided the means for its execution. On the 4th of July, 1817, ground was formally broken; and on the 26th of October, 1827, the City of New

2

York was united with the Lakes, by a stretch of navigable water extending through the Hudson River and Erie Canal, 500 miles.

Neither the City of New York, nor the Western States bordering the Lakes could reap the full advantage of this canal, without some interior, westward-extending system of corresponding improvements; accordingly, Ohio commenced her system of connections the same year in which the Erie was completed.

In 1832, the Ohio canal joining Cleveland, on Lake Erie, with Portsmouth, on the Ohio, and the Miami Canal connecting Manhattan with Cincinnati, were finished, adding 833 miles to the stretch of Canal Navigation and development, including their branches.

The States of Indiana, Illinois and Michigan followed the example of Ohio in 1836; but the financial troubles of that period delayed their works, and compelled the abandonment of some of them—whilst the superior advantages of railroads rendered it advisable to suspend others, in view of employing them in preference to canals.

However, in the first named State, the Wabash and Erie Canal was finally finished from Toledo to Evansville, passing within the State 379 miles, and in Ohio 108 miles. In Illinois, the Illinois and Michigan Canal was completed a distance of 100 miles, joining the Lakes and the Mississippi by this means, at the head waters of the Illinois river.

These elaborate works were sufficient to turn the trade of of nearly the whole of the Northwest to the City of New York; and the yearly extension of railroads in every direction, gave her a monopoly in the Export Trade of the Country, uninterrupted even yet, by any line of improvement further south.

The immediate success of the Erie canal, gave a new impulse to the commerce of New York, and as the facilities of inter-communication throughout the Western States increased, so did she advance in population, wealth and amount of exports and imports. The business of the Erie, became the measure of these, whilst it as clearly indicated the same progress in the west. The following tables show the correspondence of these movements, and in that view may be interesting.

	Canal Tolls.	Tons of Merchandise,	Value.
1820	5,244		
1830	1,056,922		
1840	1,775,749	1,417,046	66,303,893
1850	3,273,899	3,076,617	156,397,929
1856	4,108,000	4,116,082	218,327,062

	Value of Exports.		Value of Imports.
1820	11,769,511	1821	26,020,012
1830	17,666,624		38,656,064
1840	32,408,689		60,064,942
1850	47,580,357		116,667,558
1858	89,039,790		178,475,736

	City Population.		Value of Property.
1820	123,704	1824	83,075,676
1830	203,007		111,803,066
1840	312,712		252,235,515
1850	515,394		320,108,358
1855	650,000	1856	511,746,491

The combined population of these tributary States is progressively shown by the following figures.

	1820	1830	1840	1850
Ohio,	581,434	937,903	1,509,467	1,980,427
Indiana,	147,178	343,031	685,866	988,416
Illinois,	55,211	157,445	476,183	857,470
Michigan,	8,896	31,639	212,267	397,654
	792,719	1,470,018	2,893,783	4,223,967

By means of this Canal, reaching from Albany to Buffalo, and passing through the heart of the State, a disiance of 363 miles, an immense impulse was also given to State development, the influence of which was felt before it was opened for the trade of the West. Its construction was, however, designed for the latter purpose, for which no expenditure of money seemed too great. Therefore, upon its being proved too small for the wonderful increase of business, the project of widening it, at an outlay of nearly three times its original cost, was enacted into a law by the Legislature. The State has thus authorized the expenditure of $35,000,000, with a view of accommodating the trade between the East and the West. In addition to the Erie Canal, and its branches and feeders, other canals for domestic trade and development were constructed, making the entire length of artificial navigation about 990 miles.

When we simply view her water lines of communication coming from the Mississippi through Illinois to Chicago, then, diagonally through Indiana, and twice dividing Ohio, making by river and canals to the Lakes over 1600 miles; then, starting from the head waters of Lakes Superior, tracing both coasts of Lake Michigan, then through Lake Huron, Erie and Ontario, then down the St. Lawrence to Lake Champlain, over 3,000 miles, then adding the State canals and Hudson river, we find that the City of New York is the terminus of natural and artificial channels, which, if united, would make a continuous line exceeding 5,500 miles.

THE "NEW YORK CENTRAL" AND THE "NEW YORK AND ERIE" RAILROADS.

The line of the Erie Canal, as time and experiment had proved, had no rival to fear in any other State; and so long as canals were the only means of connecting the West with the East, it was secure against competition. But the early introduction of railroads changed all calculations of that nature. They were found superior for travel, more speedy for transportation, less subject to interruption by climate, and not much more costly for freighting than canals; beside all these advantages, their mode of construction allowed them to surmount by grade, or penetrate almost any physical obstacle, on a desirable route, and be entirely independent of the tortuous course and proximity of running streams.

These facts, once admitted and put in practice, by the construction of connecting roads, the Erie canal could no longer secure a monopoly; and commercial supremacy itself, might be hazarded, if not lost, when time and convenience should become the criterion for choice of ways. Under such circumstances, the dazzling prize which New York had secured, would tempt other Atlantic Cities into a struggle for its division.

Hence, New York again took the initiative, by projecting a system of railroad connections. The first of this system was the continuous Central line from Albany to Buffalo, following very near by the route of the Canal. Branches from it reached Lake Ontario at Sacketts Harbor and Cape Vincent, to the North, and to the South and towards the West, at Oswego, Great and Little Sodus, Rochester and at Lewistown. An undertaking so comprehensive would, ordinarily, have exhausted private enterprise in any state, but not so in New York, where experience had proved that a few millions invested in means of transportation would be represented by " Billions" in commerce.

With a full understanding of the immensity of the work, a third avenue, the New York and Erie Railroad, was projected and executed with special reference to the transfer and accommodation of the trade between New York City and the West. In design, comprehensiveness, execution and cost, this structure is the greatest achievement of purely commercial enterprise yet realized in this or any other country.

This road was finished in 1851. It has three outlets at tide water, and ten or more important feeders for intercepting the trade of the West, at almost every important point on Lakes Erie and Ontario, and uniting it in one immense volume upon the main trunk.

The cost of these lines and their branches, almost wholly designed and constructed with the view of localizing the Western trade in New York, is not less than $80,000,000; giving for that purpose, as well as for State development, a length of nearly 1,700 miles. In addition, for the latter design, about 1,010 miles of different lines of road have been constructed, passing through every portion of the state, and giving to almost every village, direct means of reaching the City.

The cost of this magnificent scheme of roads is estimated to reach the amount of $133,791,824. By adding to this the cost of Canals, we will find that a capital of at least $175,000,-000 has been employed in building up the commercial reputation of the State. With such power of both public and private enterprise, we need not wonder at the State's progress in agriculture, manufactures and population, nor that the City has culminated into the metropolis of America, whose commercial sway seems to be as far beyond the reach of competition, as her enterprise has yet been beyond successful imitation.

The New York Central commanded, as soon as opened, the travel between the Atlantic States and the West and Southwest, by means of its connections with the great lakes and the Western lines of improvement, and threw this travel into that City ; thus making it an *unavoidable* point in the route of almost every western and southern merchant coming East. . The result was inevitable. The merchants of New York came in contact with every class of country traders, and secured, if not all, a portion of that patronage which had been divided among the various cities hitherto more convenient, and where they had been, previously, accustomed to trade.

THE PHYSICAL CAPACITY OF PENNSYLVANIA FOR INLAND NAVIGATION AND TRADE.

The area from which Philadelphia, in early times, gathered material for an export trade, was extremely limited. To the West and Northwest, it did not extend beyond the Susquehanna. The inland navigation of this area was greatly inferior to that which terminated in the City of New York. The Schuylkill was not equal to the Mohawk, and the Lehigh not greatly superior to the Hoosic, while the Delaware held no comparison to the Hudson.

The peaceful and industrious character of the early colonists, and the manner of extinguishing and acquiring the Indian title to the land, doubtless, greatly encouraged rapid settlement. The city from the same causes, as well as from the activity of trade arising out of this immigration, grew rapidly in wealth and commercial importance. During the Revolution, both of them became important theatres of action, and the latter, especially, must have gained greatly in numbers as well as in celebrity, from the sittings of the colonial congress. Doubtless, to such causes, among others, is to be attributed the numerical superiority of the State (Virginia excepted) and the City, at the census of 1790. For many years Philadelphia, was, also the centre of wealth, aristocracy and fashion. Her import trade was, therefore, necessarily larger, and hence, her facilities for export trade greater, than those of any other port.

The earliest report of their respective populations gives New York in 1697, 4,302, and Philadelphia in 1684, 2,500. In 1771 and in 1777 the one had increased to 21,876, and the other to 23,734. The Government Census of 1790 gives Philadelphia 42,790 and New York 33,131, and their respective states 434,-373 and 340,120. No distinct tables of imports were made until a later period, but their exports in 1791 were, relatively, $3,436,093 and $2,505,465. It will be seen, that in number of population, and in amount of exports of the two states, there is a remarkable correspondence; for instance, they show an export value to each inhabitant, in the first of $7,87, and in the second $7.54. In the aggregate of exports for the five years ending with 1795, the same correspondence is maintained, and doubtless would have so continued for many years, had not the stimulant of an excessive foreign demand called the capacity of both into extraordinary activity.

The pressure of this demand did not, probably, cease prior to 1812. It may, in this connection, be interesting to the mercantile reader to contrast in figures the export trade of the two ports, from 1791, beyond the year just mentioned, up to 1820, after which time the Erie canal commenced to influence the trade of New York :

	New York.	Philadelphia.
1791	$2,505,465	$3,436,093
1792	2,535,790	3,820,662
1793	2,932,370	6,958,836
1794	5,442;183	6,643,092
1795	10,304,581	11,518,260
1796	12,208,027	17,513,866
1797	13,308,064	11,446.291
1798	14,300,892	8,915,463
1799	18,719,527	12,431,967
1800	14,045,079	11,949,679
1801	19,851,136	17,438,193
1802	13,792,276	12,677,475
1803	10,818,387	7,525,710
1804	16,081,281	11,030,157
1805	23,482,943	13,762,252
1806	21,762,845	17,574,702
1807	26,357,963	16,864,744
1808	5,606,058	4,013,350
1809	12,581,562	9,049,241
1810	17,242,330	10,993,398
1811	12,266,215	9,560,117
1812	8,961,922	5,973,750
1813	8,185,494	3,577,117
1814	209,670	
1815	10,675,373	4,593,919
1816	19,690,031	7,196,246
1817	18,707,433	8,735,592
1818	17,872,261	8,759,402
1819	13,587,378	6,293,788
1820	13,163,244	5,743,549

These tables show, that from 1791 to 1795 Philadelphia aggregated $8,656,554 more than New York; but from 1795 to 1800 the latter aggregated $10,424,323 more than the former; from 1800 to 1810, $46,647,579 more. During the next ten years, at the end of which the Erie canal affected the trade of New York, she exported $62,885,541 more than Philadelphia. The progress of population in the two States and Cities was as follows:

	1790	Per Cent.	1800	Per Cent.	1810	Per Cent.	1820
New York,	340,120	72,51	586,756	63,45	959,049	43,14	1,372,812
Pennsylvania,	434,373	38,67	602,365	34,48	810,091	29,55	1,049,458
New York City,	33,131	82.5	60,489	59.3	96,373	28.	123,706
Philadelphia,	42,790	88.6	81,005	37.4	111,210	23.2	137,097

It may also be interesting to observe the average decline of exports at Philadelphia, from 1790 to the present time, taking periods of twenty years.

	From 1791 to 1810.	From 1811 to 1830.	From 1831 to 1850
Average per year,	12,778,170	6,873,294	4,377,511

The average per annum for the seven years from 1790 to 1797, and from 1850 to 1857,

$8,762,442 - - - - $6,980,307

Showing nearly two millions in favor of the commerce of the last century.

The State maintained her superiority in population until about 1810, and the city until after 1820; yet in trade they fell behind prior to 1800, whilst responding to a call that must have brought everything to the seaboard, not prohibited by the cost of transportation.

During much of this period, Philadelphia had the advantage of the only artificial highway in the country—the Lancaster turnpike connecting her with Pittsburg. The shipping facilities of both ports were then equal, and the vast trade actually done, showed very conclusively, that neither the inland location of Philadelphia,

3

nor the navigation of the Delaware, interposed any serious obstacles to her trade. In fact, she had superior advantages,
greater wealth, greater population and the prestige in trade, and
yet she fell behind. The conclusion is therefore evident, that in
advance of the use of artificial channels for trade, New York
obtained her supremacy only by means of her superior spread of
inland navigation, which gave cheaper transportation for the
surplus products of a larger area of interior.

THE STATE WORKS OF PENNSYLVANIA.

Very early in our history, the subject of internal improvements
entered into the speculations of State economists. Possibly,
William Penn originated the first scheme for augmenting local
trade by means of canals. In much later times, however, to
the local wants of communication within the state, was added
the project of opening a water communication between the
Delaware river and the navigable water of the Ohio. A scheme
so gigantic, and against which so many obstacles were apparent,
to the most superficial observer, had many opponents. The
phlegmatic legislators of those days, required conclusive arguments
before granting authority for the commencement of a work,
rather in anticipation, than in consequence of the growth of the
State and the then sparcely populated West. The completion
of the Erie canal seemed to be conclusive on this point. In
the meantime, however, the practicability of using railroads to
surmount the Alleghany, and connect Columbia with Philadelphia, was advocated, and, unfortunately for the success of the
whole, that plan was finally adopted.

On the 4th of July, 1826, ground was ceremoniously broken
for the main line of Pennsylvania improvement; and in March
1834 it was opened for competition in a trade, for *nine* years
monopolized by New York, and which had then reached $60,-
000,000. Its capacity for competition in this trade was wholly mis-
calculated. It wanted convenient Western connections, the character of the route was unfavorable, and it was broken by railroads

which required the most expensive furniture to do even a limited trade. All freight had to be transshipped to overtop the mountains, and again to raise the Columbia grade and reach Philadelphia. The result was as widely different as success from failure. It was not only more costly, but also to the highest degree, inconvenient to the shipper of bulky products from the West. A milder climate allowed it to be serviceable later and earlier in the season than the Erie ; to this incident, and the local trade along its route, its escape from total abandonment is chiefly owing ; and to that extent only it was beneficial to the business of Philadelphia.

The import and export trade of the City, from 1830 to 1840, five years before and six after the completion of this work, will show that its effect upon her commerce was imperceptible.

	Imports.	Exports.
1830	$9,525,893	$4,291,793
1831	11,683,725	5,513,713
1832	10,048.195	3,516,066
1833	11,153,757	4,078,951
1834	10,479,268	3,989,746
1835	12,389,937	4,176,290
1836	15,068,233	3,677,607
1837	11,680,011	3,841,599
1838	9,323,840	3,477,151
1839	8,464,882	5,299,415
1840	10,342,206	6,820,145

During the construction of these works, other lines of canals were projected, consisting of the Susquehanna, North Branch, West Branch, Delaware, French Creek and Beaver divisions. These improvements were intended, strictly, for local business, and had not the failure of the main line, and consequent loss of State credit, prevented the completion of the system according to the original design, they would have accelerated the progress of State development immensely. Their construction and failure, on the contrary, entailed an immense loss and a heavy debt upon the commonwealth. This can be reckoned in dollars, but the commercial injury thus inflicted upon the State and City is beyond all calculation. Thirty years may be said to have been lost in the race for the Golden Fleece of the West—lost to

Pennsylvania, but gained by New York, making the commercial progress of the latter the most brilliant in the world, and that of the former merely an inglorious struggle to keep up appearances.

THE PROGRESS OF STATE DEVELOPEMENT AND INTERNAL IMPROVEMENT.

1. *The Coal Interests.*—About the same time that the subject of interval improvement and western connections engaged the public mind, the first Anthracite Coal was brought to Philadelphia, by a man to whose memory there is yet no public monument. In 1817, Col. George Shoemaker was enabled to sell and bestow, to a few *credulous* persons, ten loads of Anthracite Coal. Only two of these experimentors met with success, and it was not until 1825, that coal was used for the generation of Steam. Soon after this, the vast deposits of the "Black Diamond" engaged the attention of Capitalists in the City, and in 1829, speculation in Coal Lands attained a point of importance seldom reached in the progress of any excitement.

In an incredibly short time, many millions of dollars enriched the interior, and found employment in buying farming and coal lands—in locating towns never to be populated—in projecting and grading roads never to be completed—in digging canals years in advance of their demand, and in opening mines, in curious imitation of Cretan labyrinths, before the means for forwarding, or even consuming the Coal to be mined, were in existence. Almost all these early pioneers of the coal fields, were Citizens of Philadelphia, who, transported with the sudden prospect of illimitable gain, invested their money in these unopened regions of fabulous wealth. Their time, attention and Capital, were thus completely diverted from the more natural pursuits of ship-building and commercial adventures.

But the value of these coal fields advanced year by year, as their products grew in demand, until the wildest imaginings of the early adventurers are now more than realized. In 1820 but 365 tons reached tide-water, now 8,000,000 of tons give a commercial value to this single item of domestic product of $25,-000,000. But this amazing progress in production, was only made possible by constructing a system of Canals and railroads among the mines, and from them to tide-water. To accommodate, as well as accelerate, this progress, 800 miles of Canal now traverse the eastern portion of the state. These improvements were mostly made from private means, and involved the expenditure of over $127,500,000. How much of this amount was abstracted from the coffers of the mercantile classes, and consequently from commerce, must be left to conjecture.

One of the direct consequences of the coal trade, was the early impulse which it gave to investment in all kinds of manufacturing establishments in which coal, in any way, was largely consumed. It was especially instrumental in making the Eastern portion of the state the largest anthracite iron producer of the United States. Following furnaces, come Foundaries and Rolling Mills, and every other species of manufacturing in which iron was the chief material. The same influences built Cotton and Woolen Factories, and fostered all the branches of production in articles, and in machinery, incident to that business. In brief, the manufacturing celebrity of Philadelphia and her vicinity, is the most important result of the capital so liberally expended in utilizing this valuable mineral.

It is estimated that the coal fields of Pennsylvania equal one-third of her whole area. Taking this as correct, she would have out of 46,000 square miles, or 29,440,000 acres, 9,813,000 acres of coal land. The Southern, Northern and Middle Districts, comprising the Anthracite fields, are estimated at 238,280 acres, the production of which, during the last year, amounted to 6,824,854. Allowing 20 cents per ton mining license to be the measure of income, each acre, by average, would have yielded an income of about $6 00—giving $100 00 as the average value of each acre. Taking one-third of that, or $33 00 to be the standard of value, the coal lands of the State would be worth $323,829,000. Doubtless this is far below the actual value, viewing their productive capacity as a means of promoting industry and trade. If, for instance, we fix the market value of coal at $3 00 per ton, and allow the owner 20 cents per ton from that, we have $2 80 per ton for the miner, transporter and merchant ; and it only requires the production of 6,939,193 tons, at that rate, to yield $19,429,740 for interest upon the capital, $323,-829,000. That production is now far exceeded, annually.

COAL TRADE OF EASTERN PENNSYLVANIA, FROM 1820 TO 1858.

Years.	Tons.	Years.	Tons.	Years.	Tons.
1820......	365	1833......	487,784	1846......	2,374.070
1821......	1,073	1834......	376,636	1847......	2,935,249
1822......	3,720	1835......	560,758	1848......	3 168,804
1823......	6,951	1836......	684,117	1849......	3,385,415
1824......	11,108	1837......	879,444	1850......	3,555,745
1825......	34,893	1838......	738,697	1851......	4,161,443
1826......	48,047	1839......	818,402	1852......	5,327,649
1827......	63,434	1840......	868,619	1853......	5,729,131
1828......	77,516	1841......	949,963	1854......	6.650,633
1829......	112,083	1842......	1,110,426	1855......	7,288,572
1830......	174,734	1843......	1,273,670	1856......	7,695,893
1831......	176,820	1844......	1,667,372	1857......	7.307,331
1832......	363,271	1845......	2,057,754	1858......	7,654,185

2. *Manufacturing Interests.*—According to the census of 1850 there were 21,605 establishments, producing each $500 and upwards annually, engaged in Manufactures, mining and the mechanic arts, employing $94,473,810 capital, and products $155,044,910 ; of these the principals were

		No. of Establishments.	Capital Invested.	Value of Products.
1	Iron,			
	Pig Iron,	180	$8,570,425	$6,071,513
	Castings,	320	3,422,924	5,354,881
	Wrought,	131	7,620,066	8,902,907
2	Cotton,	208	4,528,995	5,322,262
3	Wollen,	380	3,005,064	5,321,866

The total, as stated above, was then, and is now, greatly below the real capital invested in, and the products of, our manufactures in this state. The following summary, taken from a recent work called " Philadelphia and its Manufactures," shows that the productions of the City and vicinity alone reach a value greatly beyond that amount. Pages 420—21.

Aggregate Value of Articles produced in Philadelphia for the year ending June 30th, 1857.

Agricultural Implements, Seeds, &c (estimated) - - - -	$500,000
Alcohol, Burning Fluid, and Camphene. - - - - - -	1,022,140
Ale, Porter, and Brown Stout. -	1,020,000
Artificial flowers. - - - -	85,000
Awnings, Bags, &c. - - -	91,750
Assaying and Refining Precious Metals, including actual expenses of U. S. Mint, $430,000. - - -	850,000
Barrels. Casks, Shooks. and Vats.	715,000
Beer. Lager and Small. - -	1,280,000
Blacking. Ink, and Lampblack, (estimated.) - - - - -	500,000
Bolts, Nuts, Screws, &c. - -	411,000
Book and Periodical Publishing, exclusive of Paper, Printing, Binding, dc. - - - - - -	18,00
Book Binding, Blank Books, and Marble Paper. - - -	1,239,000
Boots and Shoes. - - - -	4,141,000
Boxes, Packing, (estimated) -	500,000
Brass Articles. - - - -	830,000
Bread, Bakers, (including Crackers,) ship Bread, &c. - - -	$5,600,000
Bricks, Common and Pressed. -	812,000
Britannia and Plated Wares. -	380,000
Brooms, Corn and other. -	104,000
Brushes. - - - - -	225,000
Candles, Adamantine & Oleine Oils.	570,000
Caps. - - - - - -	400,000
Cards. Playing. - - - -	118.000
Carpeting, Ingrain. - - -	2,592,000
Carpeting, Rag. - - -	504,000
Carriages and Coaches. - - -	900,000
Cars and Car Wheels. - -	553,000
Chemicals, Dye-Stuffs, Chrome Colors, and Extracts. - -	3,335,000
Clothing. - - - - -	9,640,000
Coffins, Ready-made. - - -	219,000
Combs. - - - - -	150,000
Confectionery, &c. - - - -	1,020,000
Copper Work. - - - -	400,000
Cordials, Bay Water, &c. - -	200,000
Cotton and Woolen Goods, exclusive of Hosiery, Carpetings, &c.	14,813,968
Cordage, Twines, &c. - - -	810,000
Cutlery, Skates, &c. - -	150,000
Daguerreotypes, Cases, and Materials. (estimated) - - -	600,000
Edge Tools, Hammers, &c. -	127,000
Earthenware, Fire-Bricks, &c. -	647,000
Engines, Locomotive, Stationery and Fire. - - - - -	3,428,000
Engraving and Lithography. -	570,000
Envelopes and Fancy Stationery	150,000
Flooring and Planed Lumber. -	370,900
Flour. - - - - -	3,200.000
Fertilizers. - - - - -	503,000
Fringes, Tassels, and Narrow Textile Fabrics. - - - -	1,288,000
Furniture (estimated) - - -	2,500,000
Fur - - - -	350,000
Gloves, Buckskin and Kid. - -	150,000
Glue, Curled Hair &c. - -	775,000
Gold Leaf and Foil. - -	325,000
Glassware. - - - -	1,600,000
Hardware, and Iron Manufactures not otherwise enumerated. - -	1,160,000
Hats, Silk and Soft. - - -	800,000
Hose, Belting, &c. - - - -	175,000
Hosiery. - - - - -	1,808,150
Hollow-ware, exclus'e of Stoves, &c.	1,250,000
Iron, Bar, Sheet, and Forged. -	1,517,650
Jewelry, and Manufacturers of Gold.	1,275,000
Lamps, Chandeliers, and Gas Fixtures. - - - - -	1,300,000
Lasts and Boot Trees. - - .	36,000
Lead Pipe, Sheet Lead, Shot, &c.	235,000
Leather, exclusive of Morocco. -	1,610,000
Machinery. - - - - -	1,912,000
Machine Tools. - - - -	350,000
Mahogany and Sawed Lumber. -	580,000
Maps and Charts. - - -	400,000
Marble Work. - - - -	860,000
Mantillas and Corsets. - -	330,000
Matches, Friction. - - -	125.000
Medicines, Patent and Prepared Remedies. - - - -	1,300,000
Millinery Goods, including Bonnet Frames, Wire,&c., but excluding Straw Goods, Artificial Flowers	360,000
Mouldings, &c. - - -	300,000
Morrocco and Fancy Leather. -	1,156 250
Musical Instruments. - - -	485,000
Mineral Waters. - - - -	350,000
Newspapers, Daily and Weekly. -	1,370,000
Oil Cloths. - - - -	289,000
Oils, Linseed, Lard and Tallow, Rosin, and R. R. Greases. - -	2,131,230
Paints, Zinc, and Products of Paint Mills. - - - -	770,000
Paper. - - - - -	1,250.000
Paper Hangings. - - -	800,000
Paper Boxes. - - - -	175,000
Patterns. Stove and Machinery. -	115,000
Perfumery and Fancy Soaps. -	850,000
Picture and Looking-Glass Frames	750,000
Preserved Fruits, &c., (estimated)	350,000
Printing, Book and Job. - -	1,183,000
Printing Inks. - - -	160,000
Provisions—Cured Meats, Packed Beef. &c - - -	4,000,000
Rifles and Pistols. - - -	120,000
Saddles, Harness, &c. - -	1,500,000
Safes. - - - - -	150,000
Sails. - - - - -	135,000
Sash, Blinds, Doors, &c. - -	250,000
Saws. - - - - -	510,000
Scales and Balances. - -	145,000
Shirts. Collars, Bosoms, and Gentlemen's Furnishing Goods. -	1,187,500
Shovels, Spades, Hoes, &c. -	397,000
Show Cases. - - -	55,000
Sewing Silks. - - - -	812,000
Silver-ware. - - - -	450,000
Soap and Candles, exclusive of Adamantine Candles. - - -	1,487,600
Springs, Rail-road and Coach. -	238,000
Spices, Condiments, Essence of Coffee, &c - - " - -	350,000
Starch. - - - -	155,000
Steel, Spring and Cast. - -	283,500
Stoves and Grates. - -	1,250,000
Sand-stone Granite, Slate, &c. -	300,000
Straw Goods, including Hats. -	600,000
Surgical and Dental Instruments, Trusses and Artificial Limbs.	350,000
Sugar, Refined and Molasses. -	6,500,000
Teeth. Porcelain. - -	500,000
Tin, Zinc, and Sheet-Iron Ware. -	1,200,000
Tobacco Manufacturers, Cigars, Snuff, &c.	3,256,500
Trunks and Portmanteaus. -	313,000
Turnings in Wood. - - -	550,000
Type and Stereotype. - -	650,000
Umbrellas and Parasols, including Umbrella Furniture. Ivory & Bone Turning, Whalebone Cutting - - - - -	1,750,000

Upholstery, (estimated) - -	500,000
Varnishes. - - - - - -	230,000
Vessels, Masts and Spars, Blocks and Pumps, &c. - - - - -	1,760,000
Vinegar and Cider. - - -	300,000
Wagons, Carts, and Drays. - -	815,000
Watch Cases. - - - -	942,000
Whips. - - - - - - - -	175,000
Whiskey. Distilled. - - -	630,000
Whiskey, Rectified. - - - -	2,524,500
White Lead. - - - -	960,000
Willow-ware, Baskets &c. (estm'd)	120,000
Wire-work, (estimated) - -	250,000
Wooden and Cedar-ware. - -	150,000
Works in Wood not otherwise enumerated. - - - -	100,000
Miscellaneous Articles not otherwise enumerated. For particulars see INDEX, (estimated) - -	3,000,000
Total Annual product of Manufacturing Industry in Philadelphia. - - - -	**145,348,738**
Add for Leading Branches in the vicinity of Philadelphia, as before given. - - -	**26,500,000**
Total for Philadelphia and vicinity. - - - -	**$171,848,738**

"According to the Census of 1850, the average productive power of each person employed in Manufactures in Philadelphia, was about $1,100 per annum, a rate confirmed by our own investigations; and the capital invested was about one-half the aggregate of production. Assuming that these relative proportions were correct, though the aggregate amounts were manifestly erroneous, and assuming they are applicable now, the respective items would stand as follows: *Capital* invested in Manufactures in Philadelphia, **$72,500,000**; *Hands* employed, **132,000**; *Product,* **$145,348,738.**"

3. *The Railroad System of Pennsylvania.*

(Copied from Mining Journal.)

TITLES OF COMPANIES.	Total length.	Mileage in operation.	Cost.
Alleghany Valley	176	44	1,988,317
Barclay coal	16¼	16¼	438,000
Beaver Meadow	21	21	1,542,950
Branches	19	19	
Carbon Run	2½	2½	45,000
Catawissa, Williamsport and Erie	63½	63½	3,722,016
Chartiers Valley	26	26	800,000
Chester Valley	21	21	1,370,600
Chestnut Hill	3½	3½	80,000
Cleveland and Erie, (*See* OHIO, 23 m. in PA.			
Cleveland and Pittsburg, (*See* OHIO, 14 m. in PA.			
Cumberland Valley	52½	52½	1,226,675
Danville and Pottsville	31	31	500,000
Dauphin and Susquehanna	54	54	1,600,000
Delaware and Hudson Canal Co.	17	17	854,823
Branches	6	6	
Dela., Lackawanna & Western	110¾	110¾	8,701,888
Branch	2¼	2¼	
Erie and Northeast	19	19	750,000
Franklin	22	22	240,000
Gettysburg	37	9	165,000
Hanover Branch	13	13	169,445
Harrisburg and Lancaster	36	36	1,881,697
Columbia Branch	19	19	

Hazelton and Lehigh......................	14½	14½	400,000
Hempfield..............	82	35	1,388,168
Huntingdon and Broad Top..........	30½	30½ }	1,181,997
Branches............................	10¼	10¼ }	
Lackawanna................	17	9	300,000
Lackawanna and Bloomsburg........	57	57	1,650, 000
Lebanon Valley........................	53½	53½	2,800,000
Lehigh and Susquehanna	20	20	1,250,000
Lehigh Valley..........................	46	46	3,276,523
Little Schuylkill......	28	28 }	1,407,651
Branches............................	5	5 }	
Lykens Valley............................	16	16	443,000
Mauch Chunk and Summit Hill,.....	8	8 }	1,000,900
Branches............................	21	21 }	
Mine Hill and Schuylkill Haven, ...	25	25 }	2,400,000
Branches.............................	90	90 }	
Mount Carbon............................	1¼	1¼ }	198,481
Branches............................	6	6 }	
Mount Carbon and Port Carbon......	3½	3½	
Northern Central, (*See Md.* 96 m. in Pa.)			
North Pennsylvania.....................	55½	55½ }	5,106,342
Doylestown Branch................	10¼	10¼ }	
Shimersville Branch..............	1¾	1¾ }	
Pennsylvania......................	248	248 ⌉	18,994,719
Blairsville Branch.................	8	3	
Indiana Branch.....................	13	18	
Hollidaysburg Branch............	6	6 ⌋	
Alleghany Portage................	28½	28½	2,100,027
Philadelphia Division.............	87	81	5,277,278
Pennsylvania Coal.....................	40	47	3,800,000
Philadelphia and Balt. Central.......	16	13	600,000
Phila., Germantown and Nor........	17	17 }	1,710,812
Germantown Branch..............	4	4 }	
Philadelphia and Reading.............	93	93 }	19,004,180
City Branch.........................	5	5 }	
Philadelphia and Sunbury.............	33	33	1,348,812
Philadelphia and Trenton.............	28	28	1,000,000
Philadelphia, Wilmington and Baltimore (*See* Md. 19 m. in Pa.)			
Pittsburg and Connellsville...........	148	48	1,819,155
Pittsburg. Ft. Wayne and Chicago..	465	383	11,718,512
Pittsburg and Steubenville............	42	42	2,800,000
Schuylkill Valley	25	25	450,000
Sunbury and Erie......	270	40	3,666,294
Tioga	29¾	29¾	1,093,263
Treverton and Mahanoy................	14	14	700,000
Westchester.............................	9	9	165,000
Westchester, Media and Phila........	26	19	700,000
Williamsport and Elmira..............	78	78	3,464,454
Wrightsville, York and Gettysburg.	12½	12½	433,530
Sundry Coal Railroads, etc., not otherwise accounted for, say......	300	300	6,000,000
*Total...................................	3,461	2,780	$135,724,609

* Length of coal roads 1,564 miles.

4

4. The Canal System of Pennsylvania.

	Miles.	Cost.
*Schuylkill Navigation Co.,	108	$10,950,000
*Lehigh Canal and Improvements,	71	4,455,000
*Delaware Division, (State,)	60	2,200,000
*Eastern do do	46	1,737,236
*Susquehanna,	41	897,160
*Lower North Branch,	73	1,598,379
*Upper North Branch,	94	4,500,000
*Union	99	5,000,000
*Wisconisco,	12	381,836
*Morris,	102	5,612,000
*Delaware and Hudson (estimated)	108	2,500,000
Juniata Division, (state)	130	3,570,016
Western do do	105	3,095,522
West Branch, do	72	2,832,083
French Creek, do	45	817,779
Erie and Beaver,	136	
Lackawaxen,	22	
Bald Eagle,	25	
Tide Water,	45	
Conestoga,	18	
Codoris,	11	
Franklin,	22	
	1446	

SUMMARY OF THE PRESENT ELEMENTS OF STATE PROSPERITY.

Assuming that our calculations are sufficiently correct to give a general idea of the elements which impart to the State its commercial value in the community of nations, we will group together those which are the most prominent.

The coal production of 1858, 7,654,185, say	$25,000,000
Productions in Iron, Cotton and Woollen, outside of the city	30,000,000
†Miscellaneous production outside of the city	80,000,000
Product of manufactures in the city and vicinity	171,848,738
Agricultural production (estimated)	85,000,000
Lumber "	10,000,000
	401,848,738

* Canals connected with the Anthracite Coal trade, Total length 815 miles: cost $39,831,611.
† Inclusive of Live Stock.

Capital representation in coal lands	$323,829,000
" " *in farm lands	500,000,000
" " in manufactures, outside the city	80,000,000
" " in city and vicinity	72,500,000
" " *Real and personal estate, exclusive of farms	800,000,000
" " in Railroads	135,724,609
" " in Canals	62,500,000

The State has, according to decennial increase a population of about 2,825,000, and her improvements completed and projected pass through or upon the borders of sixty out of her sixty-five counties, and if in one line would extend over 4,000 miles.

The City of Philadelphia is the commercial focus of the State, and contains a population nearly equal to one-fourth of that of the whole State. According to the ratio of increase previous to 1850, it should now be 600,000. She has the termini of twelve railroads within her corporate limits, radiating 880 miles, representing a capital of $70,878,744, and earning a gross income of $11,275,917.

During the past eight years her imports and exports have been as follows:

	Imports.	Exports.
1850	$13,381,459	$4,669,910
1851	14,871,992	5,968,071
1852	16,113,166	5,994,554
1853	21,993,137	8,400,482
1854	17,800,210	7,628,623
1855	15,104,478	6,935,389
1856	18,128,314	7,899,929
1857	17,128,386	6,035,510
1858	12,892,215	5,662,384

In addition to the official returns of imports, it is estimated, by intelligent authority, that the merchants of Philadelphia import through New York and Boston, an average annual value of $6,000,000.

STATE DEVELOPMENT ENGROSSED CAPITAL TO THE PREJUDICE OF COMMERCE.

In considering the accumulation of such vast elements of greatness, the result of domestic industry and enterprise, all regret over the declension of foreign commerce would be out of

---

* The Secretary of the United States Treasury valued the Real and Personal Estate, in 1856, at $1,031,731,304.

place. Agriculture, mining and manufacturing demanded the capital and whole energies of our people, and placed the successful pursuit of commerce beyond the scope of cotemporaneous enterprise. Nature, as well as the *instinct of capital*, directed the successive steps of progress.

The native fuel of the forest was fast giving way before the clearing axe. The fireside and the workshop demanded a new source of supply, where tillage was impossible and the source inexhaustible. This was found beneath the soil and stored under mountains far from the main points of consumption. To mine and transport it, machinery and roads had to be employed. These again, called into existence furnaces, foundaries, rolling mills and machine shops, railroads, canals and manufactories, all of which were the acting and reacting consequents of each other, and all, therefore, naturally uniting the links of progress from the first use of coal, to the employment of capital in every ramification of production, in which it has any agency.

Commerce could not have produced these results—and the wants of the age demanded them—but out of and upon them a commercial power can be reached that should not fear comparison.

It will be seen that the mercantile classes of Philadelphia were irresistably attracted to the interior, spending both energy and capital to the detriment of exterior trade. Thus far all has been well. The fabric of State resources has been reared upon indestructable foundations, and the city has made rapid strides towards pre-eminence. Even in comparison with her commercial neighbor she has the advantage of a more rapid progress within the last fifteen years, viz :

	1820 to 1830.	to 1840.	to 1850.
Philad'a from	" 36 per ct.	" 33 per ct.	" 58 per ct.
New York,	" 65 "	" 54 "	" 65 "

being 25 per cent. increase in favor of Philadelphia, to 11 per cent. in favor of New York, from 1840 to 1850. If the same rate of increase is maintained until 1860, the per centage of the former would stand at 83, and the latter at 76.

However pleasing the reflection may be, that all this has been accomplished without the direct aid of foreign commerce, yet it affords no ground for exultation. Pennsylvania was the great magazine of that mineral wealth which the wants of the age required to be utilized. She had but to unlock her treasures and take profit from the growth of demand. But in this progress of the "manifest destiny" of State development is to be found a substantial vindication for the mercantile classes of Philadelphia, to whom the neglect of commerce would have been, otherwise, as discreditable as it would have been injurious.

Such, then, were the potential influences, which, for the time, controlled capital against taking early steps to supply the deficiencies of the State works. The time had arrived, however, when this could no longer be deferred, and yet be excusable. The advanced state of every interior interest made the task possible, as well as necessary, in order to secure the advantages of what had already been done. But in addition to this, the merchants of New York had not been satisfied to rest their ambition and enterprise upon the natural and constructed scope of navigation furnished by the great Lakes and the St. Lawrence, the Hudson river and the Erie canal; they were grasping at every point North, South, East and West, with iron arms, and dispatching steamships to every important port on the Eastern and Western coast of the Atlantic. To cope with them and prevent a total abandonment of commerce, it was necessary to adopt the same means; and the point at which to begin was plainly the construction of a railway to the West.

THE ROADS CONNECTING PHILADELPHIA WITH THE WEST.

1. *The Pennsylvania Central.*—When it is remembered that the commerce of Philadelphia had reached a point of actual insignificance, it becomes apparent that the means to build this road were not furnished from the profits of foreign trade, but it was rather an extension of a home system made possible from the profits of home enterprise. A distinct interest having absorbed commercial capital, a Western road had to be the antecedent, instead of being the consequent of commercial success —it must build up and maintain, not proceed out of, and extend foreign trade.

The difficulties which surrounded this enterprise at the outset were, therefore, of no ordinary character. Had the State canal been successful, there would have been neither delay nor difficulty; both means and disposition would have stood ready to second the enterprise. Hence years passed in mere discussion, and it was not commenced until commercial obliteration was threatened to Philadelphia. To prevent this, the Merchants of Philadelphia, at last, aroused themselves to the task of procuring the requisite means for the undertaking. Immediately after the charter of incorporation had received legal existence, active exertions were made, by a committee of Merchants, to obtain assistance from the Citizens, as well as from the corporate authorities of Philadelphia. With a liberality, which proved the deep importance of the work to the vital interests of the City, she became responsible for two and a half millions of the stock.

This gave a foundation which made success certain. It was commenced in 1847, and in running order in 1853. Thus the "gate of the west" was again connected with Philadelphia, but this time by a magnificent railway, unbroken and substantial, a monumental enterprise, requiring no sculptured words to perpetuate the memory of its projectors.

The language of eulogy may be inappropriate when the simple statement of facts carry all the praise that merit can demand. Those facts are patent in the progress of this road, from its comprehensive plan of structure, to its faithful execution—in every part exhibiting the perfect adaptation of means to ends, and the highest achievement of engineering skill in subduing physical obstacles. In system of arrangement, in the conduct of its ponderous business, in its freedom from accident and in financial credit, it has reason to fear no rivalry, if the past can give security for the future.

The route is on the diameter line from the seaboard to the west. Passing through the centre of the State, it drains from either side, and unites in its constant stream of food for man, the products of fertile vallies, with those of Iron, Coal and Lumber, from exhaustless mines and mountain forests. From its western terminus, "the Birmingham of America," railroad connections unite with navigable rivers in giving it the natural command of every important depot of the rich products of western thrift. By referring to the map, Pittsburg will appear to be the highest northern centre to the radii of which each west- ward, southward and northward extension adds only length to reach the east, without deflection, after leaving this common centre. Hence, from Tennessee in the South, Missouri in the West, and Wisconsin in the North, the Pennsylvania Central offers the shortest route for transportation and the most convenient for travel.

The saving of distance and consequently of time and cost by this road, can be made more intelligible by the following tables, than by a written statement; they are copied from " Phil- adelphia and its Manufactures," to the author of which, the business men of Philadelphia owe a debt of gratitude which should give the book a circulation, throughout the country, of tens of thousands.

DISTANCE TABLE.

	Cleaveland	Cincinnati	Indiana- polis.	Chicago.	St. Louis.
From Philadelphia via. Penna. Cen- tral to Pittsburg; thence by short- est route to	501	703	746	851	1,000
From New York via. Hudson River to Piermont, and the Erie R. R. to Dunkirk468 miles,thence by short- est railroad route to	612	867	893	954	1,154
Again, from New York via. Hudson River R. R. to Albany, thence by R. R. to Buffalo 442 miles, thence as above to	625	880	906	967	1.167
From Boston via. Western R. R. to Albany and Buffalo 498 miles, thence as above to	618	936	962	1,023	1,223

Hence, it is manifest that Philadelphia has considerable ad- vantage over New York and Boston, in nearness to the prin- cipal centres of trade in the West. The saving in distance will be regarded as an important one by the weary traveler, while its effects in reducing the cost of transportation will be shown here- after. It is true, New York has a shorter route to the places named than by the above-mentioned railroads; but that is, *via Philadelphia and Pittsburg.* Pennsylvania is truly the Keystone State; and those who would pass and repass from the West to the East, may congratulate themselves that their most direct route carries them over a railroad so well managed as the

Pennsylvania Central, and through a city so beautiful as Phila-delphia.

A Table showing the saving on a ton (2,240 lbs.) of first class freight, by shipping from Philadelphia instead of New York or Boston:

	New York.		Boston.	
	Summer.	Winter.	Summer.	Winter.
To Columbus, Ohio,	$7 39	$6 72	$8 51	$8 96
" Dayton, "	7 39	6 72	8 51	8 96
" Cincinnati, "	7 39	6 72	8 51	8 96
" Indianapolis, Ind.,	6 27	6 72	7 39	8 96
" Terre Haute, "	5 15	6 72	7 39	8 96
" Fort Wayne, "	4 03	6 50	4 03	8 74
" Lafayette, "	3 58	6 05	4 70	8 29
" Louisville, Ky.,	4 03	6 72	5 15	8 96
" St. Louis, Missouri,	2 24	6 72	6 27	8 96
" Cairo,	45	6 72	4 48	8 96
" Cleveland, Ohio,	1 79	3 36	2 91	5 60
" Chicago, Ill.,	1 79	4 48	1 79	4 48

The same author remarks, that "the advantage in shipping from Philadelphia to Pittsburg, and thence by the Ohio river to Cincinnati and Louisville, over shipping to those points by the Northern railroad lines, amounts in addition to the saving stated above, to about $5 per ton on first class goods, $4 on second, $3 on third class, and $2 on very heavy goods; while to Nash-ville, Memphis, Cairo and St. Louis, and all points south of New Albany, Ind., the additional saving is nearly double this amount—that is, about $10 per ton on first class goods, $8 on second, $6 on third, and about $3 per ton on fourth class. It is thus evident, as experienced shippers know, that freight from the West, bound for European markets, can be brought to Phila-delphia, and shipped hence, landing it at its destined ports abroad, at cheaper paying rates than by way of New York. Indeed, the leading products of the West—for instance, flour, the products of the hog, whiskey, &c., can be shipped to Phila-delphia and hence at least half the distance to Liverpool, for the cost of transporting them to New York. Further, in view of the facts stated, it is also obvious, that a Western merchant, purchasing goods in Philadelphia, may have his preference rewarded by a saving in the cost of transporting them home. The only practical question, then, for him to consider is, *whether it is probable he can make his purchases in the Philadelphia market as cheaply as in any other;* for, supposing the terms to be the same, he will, nevertheless, by doing so, obtain an advantage."

2. *The Sunbury and Erie Railroad* —But even this improvement is not all : Another important work is on the eve of completion to further the interests of commerce.

The Sunbury and Erie Railroad, first organized in 1837, is again in progress of construction, after twenty years of unpardonable neglect. It was projected to open the Northern counties of the State to settlement, and develope their wealth of mineral and agricultural resources, and when finished will form a continuous line of road from the City of Erie to Philadelphia, the entire distance being four hundred and twenty-five miles.

The physical disposition of the route renders it practicable on a grade greatly in advantage of every other Northern route having the same termination ; and its connections are such as to allow an unbroken guage, without necessity of transhipment throughout its entire distance. New York has sought to reach the same terminus, the harbor of Erie, by a road costing nearly $34,000,000, in preference to terminating only at Dunkirk, within her own territory, although to reach the former point, the distance of forty-seven miles was added, making the length of the road over five hundred miles, and with one break of guage between Dunkirk and Erie.

The Sunbury and Erie, with all its connections Eastward to Philadelphia, will not represent a capital beyond $15,000,000, will be seventy-five miles shorter, and have an unbroken guage, to compete with the greater cost, greater distance, and two transhipments of the New York and Erie.

The importance of this connection to Philadelphia, and its means for successful competition with the Northern roads, will make the following tables of comparison interesting. They were prepared nearly six years since, but doubtless have not, or will not, become inapplicable to the road now in progress.

1st. The New York and Erie route.

From Erie to State Line, 6 feet guage, . . 19 miles.
" State Line to Dunkirk, 4 ft. 10 in. guage, . 28 "
" Dunkirk to Sufferns 6 ft. guage, . . 427 "
" Sufferns to Jersey City, by Patterson, now
    Union Road, 6 ft. guage, . . . 32 "
" Jersey City to New York, by Ferry, . . 1 "
                                   ——
                                 507 "

With three transhipments, viz: at State Line, Dunkirk and Jersey City.

2d. Buffalo and Albany route.

From Erie to State Line 6 ft. guage, . . . 19 miles.
" State Line to Buffalo 4 ft. 10 in. guage, . 69 "
" Buffalo to Albany 4 ft. 8½ in. guage, . . 328 "
" Albany to New York, (Hudson River R. R.,) 144 "
                                 ——
                                 560 "

With three transhipments, viz: at State Line, Buffalo and Albany.

3d. Sunbury and Erie Railroad route.

From Erie to Philadelphia, 4 ft. 8½ in. guage the
    entire distance, ... 428 miles.
                               ——

viz: from Erie to Williamsport, . . . 240 "
" " Williamsport to Tamaqua, . . 90 "
" " Tamaqua to Philadelphia, . . 98 "

Or from Erie to Philadelphia, via Williamsport,
    thence down the Susquehanna to Harris-
    burg, thence to Philadelphia, . . . 437 "

Or from Erie to Harrisburg as above, and from
    thence to Philadelphia through Reading, by
    the Lebanon Valley road, . . . 444 "

By the estimate, that every transhipment is equal to the cost of transporting an equal amount of merchandise for fifty miles, the length of the 1st and 2d routes would be increased to 657, and 710 respectively, the Sunbury remaining the same. In addition to this, another advantage results from the difference in the ascending and descending grades on the following routes, viz:

New York and Erie, ... 12,675 feet.
Buffalo and Albany, ... 11,200 "
Sunbury and Erie, ... 8,569 "

Assuming the rise and fall of sixty feet to be equal to one mile of distance on the level, the relative distance would finally stand thus: 1st. 868 miles. 2d. 897. **3d.** 570.

The summing up of these advantages in the shape of propositions stands thus: 1st. That the Sunbury and Erie route is the shortest in actual distance between the Lakes and the Atlantic. 2d. That it crosses the Alleghany mountains with better grades than any other line now completed or projected. 3d. That in equated distance (allowing for transhipment and rise and fall) it exhibits advantages which defy competition.

In this connection we must not overlook the completion of the Fort Wayne and Chicago road, uniting the latter city with Philadelphia by one continuous railway. As an accessory this road, under the wise management which distinguishes the Central, is calculated to exert an influence upon the destinies of the city, second only to that of the Central itself. Unitedly they proffer to that vast region, composed of Ohio, Indiana, Illinois, Wisconsin, Iowa and Missouri, greater facilities for transportation and travel, than any other routes eastward. These advantages are self-evident, and to make them the foundation for commercial operations extending to millions, it is but necessary to convince the business men of these States, that Philadelphia has all the requisite facilities to dispose of their consignments, and upon terms equally satisfactory with those to be obtained in any other Eastern city. Parenthetically, it may be remarked that the grain trade of Chicago in 1840, amounted to 10,000 bushels, in 1850 to 1,830,938; in 1856 to 21,583,221, and in 1858 to 20,035,166 bushels.

To the South and South-west, Philadelphia naturally stands in a position to command a large share in the trade which must seek the Philadelphia, Wilmington and Baltimore road. With this road connections have been made through Virginia to Memphis, Tennessee; also South to Charleston, South Carolina;

Augusta and Atalanta, Georgia; and Montgomery, Alabama; and from the latter a road is in a state of forwardness to Pensacola, Florida. The most of these roads are calculated to attract the travel which has hitherto gone by sea, very little of it reaching Philadelphia. It remains to be seen, whether Philadelphians will take means to extend their business relations in these States, and prepare themselves to take advantage of the trade that must follow the development of the vast country through which these roads pass.

THE AREA, POPULATION, WEALTH AND TRADE OF THE WEST AND NORTHWEST.

It will thus be perceived that Philadelphia, backed by all the elements of State wealth and resources is now prepared, so far as inland means of transportation are concerned, to join in a trade the future growth of which neither figures nor imagination can magnify beyond what may be realized, even in the next half a century. To give some idea, however, of its present and future importance, we transfer the following tables to these pages:

Superficial Area of the Northwestern States and Territories.

STATES, ETC.	SUPERFICIES.
Ohio,	39,964 square miles.
Indiana,	33,809 "
Michigan,	56,243 "
Illinois,	55,405 "
Wisconsin,	53,924 "
Missouri,	67,380 "
Iowa,	50,914 "
Minnesota,	75,464 "
Dacotah Territory, (not organized,)	90,561 "
Nebraska Territory,	335,882 "
Kansas Territory,	174,798 "
Total area,	974,344 "

Population of this area in 1820, 1830, 1840, 1850 *and* 1858,
and the Average Population to the square mile at each of
these periods.

ABSOLUTE POPULATION.

States and Territories.	1820	1830	1840	1830	1858
Ohio,...............	581,434	937,903	1,519,467	1,977,031	*2,450,000
Indiana, ...	147,178	343,031	685,866	988,734	*1,300,000
Michigan,.........	8,896	31,639	212,267	397,654	*650,000
Illinois,............	55,211	157,545	476,183	851,298	*1,550,000
Wisconsin,.......	......	......	30,945	304,226	*650,000
Missouri, ...	66,586	140,445	383,702	682,043	*1,000,000
Iowa,...............	......	......	43,112	192,214	*600,000
Minnesota,.......	......	......	......	6,000	†153,000
Dacotah Ter.,....	......	......	......	......	*5,000
Nebraska Ter.,..	......	......	......	......	*20,000
Kansas Ter.,......	......	......	......	......	*75,000
Totals,..........	859,385	1,910,473	3,321,542	5,397,200	8,453,000

Increase of population from 1820 to 1830,............................1,051,088
   Do   do   1830 to 1840,............................1,411,069
   Do   do   1840 to 1850,............................2,075,658
   Do   do   1850 to 1858,............................3,055,800

Increase in thirty-eight years,..7,593,615
Per centage in thirty-eight years,..................................... 889

AVERAGE POPULATION TO THE SQUARE MILE.

States and Territories.	1820.	1830.	1840.	1850.	1858.
Ohio,....	14.5	23.4	38.	49.4	61.3
Indiana,...............................	4.3	10.5	20.2	29.2	38.4
Michigan,............................	0.15	0.56	3.7	7.	9.
Illinois, ...	1.	2.9	8.	15.	27.9
Wisconsin, ...	0.	0.	0.056	5.6	12.
Missouri,............................	1.	2.1	5.9	10.5	15.3
Iowa, ...	0.	0.	0.84	3.7	11.7
Minnesota,..........................	0.	0.	0.	0.08	2.
Dacotah Ter.,.......................	0.	0.	0.	0.	0.055
Nebraska Ter.,......................	0.	0.	0.	0.	0.059
Kansas Ter.,.........................	0.	0.	0.	0.	0.65

Average population of whole area to square mile, 1820,.......... .088
  Do   do   do   do   1830,.........1.9
  Do   do   do   do   1840,.........3.4
  Do   do   do   do   1850,.........5.53
  Do   do   do   do   1858,.........8.67

* Estimated.   † Official.

Taxable Property, Real and Personal, in the several States named.

States.	1840	1850	1855	1858
Ohio,..........	$128,353,657	$439,996,340	$837,425,743	$860,877,354
Indiana,......	107,037,317	152,870,399	290,418,148	301,858,474
Michigan,...	37,833,024	29,384,270	120,362,474	137,663,009
Illinois, ...	*74,284,000	114,782,645	333,287,174	407,477,367
Wisconsin, ..	*5,580,000	26,715,525	72,912,318	87,512,917
Missouri, ...	*55,296,000	97,595,463	223,948,221	268,789,211
Iowa,.........	*6,708,000	22,623,334	116,895,390	210,944,583
Minnesota,...................		1,182,060	9,031,157	23,347,701
Total,......	$415,091,998	$885,120,036	$2,004,280,625	$2,298,470,616

Add for Kansas, Nebraska, and Dacotah, estimated,...... 25,000,000

Making an aggregate valuation of $2,323,470,616
Increase from 1840 to 1850,.........................$470,028,038
    do.   1850 to 1855,........................1,119,160,589
    do.   1855 to 1858,...................... 319,189,991

Taxable Property, Real and Personal, in the Eastern and Middle States.

	1850	1855	1858
Eastern States,..........	$1,012,985,902	$1,214,356,926	$1,374,340,682
Middle States,...........	1,593,256,934	2,788,344,883	2,933,526,584

Superficial Area and Population to the Square Mile in the Eastern and Middle States, and in France, Great Britain and Belgium.

1.—SUPERFICIAL AREA.

E. States, (incl. Me., N. H.. Vt., Mass., R. I., and Ct..) 65,038 sq. miles.
Middle States, (incl. N Y., N. J., Pa., Del., and Md.,) 114,564   "
France, (incl. Corsica,)......................................207,149   "
Great Britain, (excl. of Ireland,)............................. 89,644   "
Belgium, ... 11,402   "

2.—ABSOLUTE POPULATION.

	1840.	1845.	1850.	1855.
Eastern States,..........	2,234,822	2,492,986	2,728,116	3,000,921
Middle States,..........	5,074,364	5,822,337	6,624,988	7,315,546
France,...................	34,230,178	34,921,333	35,781,628	36,039,364
Great Britain,..........	18,529,316	19,581,723	20,816,351	22,080,399
Belgium, ...	4,073.162	4,209,984	4,359,932	4,530,228

* Estimated.

3.—Average Proportion to the Square Mile.

	1840.	1845.	1850.	1855.
Eastern States,	34.4	38.3	41.9	45.4
Middle States,	44.3	50.8	57.9	63.9
France,	165.2	168.6	172.7	173.9
Great Britain,	206.8	218.2	232.2	246.3
Belgium,	357.2	369.2	382.4	397.3

The following table shows what the population of our Northwestern States and Territories will be when its density shall reach that of the Districts and Countries named above:

Same density with Eastern States,		44,225,218
Do.	do. Middle States,	62,260,582
Do.	do. France	162,338;412
Do.	do. Great Britain,	239,980,927
Do.	do. Belgium,	386,396,871

American Lakes.

	Length, miles.	Breadth, miles.	Area, sq. miles.
Superior,	420	120	32,100
Michigan,	320	70	21,900
Huron,	270	145	18,750
St. Clair,	25	18	300
Erie,	250	45	9,300
Ontario,	190	40	7,300
St. Lawrence River,	700	...	...

To show the growth of the lake trade, and to give some idea of its future, we give the following figures; during the past fifteen years the trade of the lakes has grown from $65,000,000 in 1841, to $608,310,000, in 1856, or to more than double the entire foreign commerce of the country. The whole of this aggregate, with the exception of $42,260,000, came through the following ports:

Buffalo,	$303,023,000	Milwaukie,	$35,000,000
Chicago,	223,898,000	Maumee,	94,107,000
Cleveland,	162,185,000	Sandusky,	59,966,000
Detroit,	140,000,000	Oswego,	146,235,000

The tonnage entered and cleared at the lake ports in 1856, was:

	ENTERED.		CLEARED.	
	Steam.	Sail.	Steam.	Sail.
American,	1,434,779	464,822	1,482,548	438,862
Foreign,	397,587	174,619	398,702	166,010
Total	1,832,366	639,441	1,881,250	604,872

Comparative Statements of the Inland and Western Trade of New York and Pennsylvania, carried to and from Tide-water, by through Canals and Railroads, showing the influence of this trade upon the commerce, wealth and population of the two States, and the Cities of New York and Philadelphia.

It is not claimed that the following calculations are entirely correct, but sufficiently so to answer our purpose, viz: to show the very small portion of the Western trade which has yet reached Philadelphia by means of her connection with the West. The value of the total tonnage movement on canals and railroads, where no reported values are found, is obtained by multiplying the yearly returns of the aggregate tonnage by 53, as the average value per ton:

Total value of the canal movement in New York, from 1824 to 1851, - - - - - - - - -					$1,650,500,000
Total value of the canal movement in New York in 1852,					196,603,517
"	"	N. Y., E. and C. R. R.	"	"	40,000,000
"	"	Canals	"	1853,	207,179,570
"	"	R. R.	"	"	52,500,000
"	"	Canals,	"	1854,	210,248,312
"	"	R. R.	"	"	68,500,000
"	"	Canals,	"	1855,	204,390,147
"	"	R. R.	"	"	80,000,000
"	"	Canals,	"	1856,	218,327,062
"	"	R. R.	"	"	91,000,000
"	"	Canals,	"	1857,	177,235,233
"	"	R. R.	"	"	96,000,000

$3,292,478,841

Being unable to find any reliable statistics of the State canal, by reason of its having two outlets, one by the Columbia railroad, and the other, by the C. and Tide-water canal, we can only give the movement on the Pennsylvania Central from 1853.

Total amount by Pennsylvania Central Railroad, 1853,			-	-	$4,617,784
"	"	"	1854,	-	-	7,551,334
"	"	"	1855,	-	-	12,413,554
"	"	"	1856,	-	-	14,345,245
"	"	"	1857,	-	-	16,379,650

FOREIGN COMMERCE OF THE TWO PORTS.

	IMPORTS.		EXPORTS.	
	New York,	Philadelphia,	New York.	Philadelphia.
1821 -	$26,020,012 -	$ 8,158,922	$12,124,645 -	$7,391,767
1822 -	33,912,453 -	11,874,170	15,405,694 -	9,047,802
1823 -	30,601,455 -	13,696,770	21,089,696 -	9,617,192
1824 -	37,783,747 -	11,865,531	22,309,362 -	9,364,893
1825 -	50,024,973 -	15,041,797	34,032,279 -	11,269,981
1826 -	34,728,664 -	13,551,779	19,437,229 -	8,331,722
1827 -	41,441,832 -	11,212,935	24,614,035 -	7,575,833
1828 -	39,117,016 -	12,884,408	22,135,487 -	6,051,480
1829 -	34,972,493 -	10,100,152	17,609,600 -	4,089,935
1830 -	38,656,064 -	9,525,893	17,666,624 -	4,291,793
1831 -	57,291,727 -	11,673,755	26,142,719 -	5,503,713
1832 -	42,542,012 -	10,048,195	22,792,599 -	3,516,066
1833 -	56,527,976 -	11,153,757	24,703,903 -	4,078,951
1834 -	72,724,210 -	10,479,268	23,842,736 -	3,989,746
1835 -	87,734,844 -	12,389,937	29,451,192 -	4,176,290
1836 -	117,700,917 -	15,068,233	27,668,159 -	3,677,607
1837 -	78,543,706 -	11,680,011	25,459,627 -	3,841,599
1838 -	68,159,360 -	9,323,840	21,654,765 -	3,477,151
1839 -	99,483,414 -	15,037,420	31,946,474 -	5,299,415
1840 -	60,064,942 -	8,464,882	32,408,689 -	6,820,145
1841 -	75,358,283 -	10,342,206	30,792,780 -	5,152,501
1842 -	57,446,081 -	7,381,770	25,467,316 -	3,753,894
1843 -	31,112,227 -	2,755,958	15,972,084 -	2,354,948
1844 -	64,528,188 -	7,217,238	29,722,803 -	3,535,256
1845 -	69,897,405 -	8,156,446	33,554,776 -	3,574,363
1846 -	73,531,611 -	7,989,393	33,646,006 -	4,751,005
1847 -	83,075,296 -	9,586,126	46,586,635 -	8,541,167
1848 -	92,947,176 -	12,147,000	49,742,238 -	5,732,333
1849 -	91,374,584 -	10,644,803	42,788,237 -	5,543,421
1850 -	116,667,558 -	13,381,459	47,580,357 -	4,669,910
1851 -	141,546,538 -	14,168,761	68,104,542 -	5,101,969
1852 -	132,329,306 -	14,785,917	74,042,581 -	5,522,449
1853 -	178,270,999 -	18,834,410	66,030,355 -	6,255,229
1854 -	195,427,933 -	21,359,306	105,551,740 -	9,846,810
1855 -	164,776,511 -	15,309,935	96,414,808 -	5,985,125
1856 -	210,162,254 -	16,590,045	109,848,509 -	7,043,408
1857 -	236,493,485 -	17,128,386	119,197,301 -	5,662,384

RECEIPTS OF BREADSTUFFS.

	Flour, bbls.	Wheat, bus.	Corn, bus.
Receipts of Flour at New York by Canals alone, from 1853 to 1857,	7,569,406	35,923,485	40,479,997
Receipts by Pennsylvania Central Railroad, from 1853 to 1857,	1,417,740	*4,460,828	*6,501,658

Total cost of the Erie canal, when the enlargement is completed, and the two railroads, is estimated at $115,000,000.

Total cost of the Pennsylvania connection with the West, now owned by the Pennsylvania Central Railroad Company,

* No distinct returns. These figures are taken from the Grain Measurers' Report.

$27,266,981. To which, add cost of Sunbury and Erie, when completed.

	1850.	1856.
Value of Real and Personal Estate in the State of New York - - - -	$1,080,309,216	$1,364,154,625
Value of Real and Personal Estate in the State of Pennsylvania - - -	729,144,998	1,031,731,304

	1825.	1857.
Valuation of Real and Personal Property in New York City and Brooklyn -	106,000,000	620,000,000
Valuation of Real and Personal Property in Philadelphia - - - -	37,280,441	162,979,653

	1830.	1840.	1850.	1858.
Population of N. Y.,	1,913,006	2,428,921	3,097.390	*3,980,000
" of Pennsylvania,	1,348,233	1,724,033	2,311.786	*2,800,000
" of City N. Y.,	202,589	312.710	†653,000	†1,046,000
" of City Philad.,	167,325	258,037	408,762	*650,000
Foreign population of New York City,			235,733	
" " Philadelphia,			121,697	

Average daily arrival of emigrants in New York, 1,000.

STEAM-VESSELS EMPLOYED IN THE TRADE OF NEW YORK.

U. S. MAIL BOATS.

		No.	Tonnage.
Collins' Line, . .	Adriatic, Atlantic, Baltic, . .	3	9,727
Havre " . .	. Arago, Fulton, ...	2	4,548
Vanderbilt, Bremen, .	North Star, Ariel, Vanderbilt, .	3	6,523
U. S. M. S. S. Company, .	Illinois, Empire City, Philadelphia, Granada, Moses Taylor, Star of the West, ...	6	8,544
N. Y. Havana and N. O.,	Black Warrior, Cahawba, . .	2	3,119
" " Mobile,	Quaker City, ...	1	1,428
" Savannah, .	. Alabama, Florida, Augusta, Star of the South, ...	4	4,795
" Charleston, .	Columbia, Nashville, Marion, James Adger, ...	4	4,680
" Virginia, .	. Roanoke, Jamestown, . .	2	2,371

TRANS-ATLANTIC STEAMSHIPS.

					No.	Tonnage.
Cunard	Line,	Liverpool,	(sidewheel,)	British,	4	10,360
Scotch	"	Glasgow,	(screw,)	"	3	6,512
Irish	"	Cork,	"	"	2	2,600
Cunard	"	Havre,	"	"	5	11,800
French	"	"	"	French,	3	4,500
Old Havre	"	"	(sidewheel,)	American,	3	7,200
Vanderbilt	"	"	"	"	3	7,600
Independent	"	"	"	"	1	1,800
Bremen	"	Bremen,	"	"	2	4,000
Belgian	"	Antwerp,	(screw,)	Belgian,	5	12,590
Hamburg	"	Hamburg,	"	German,	2	2,400
					60	117,195

* Estimated.   † Including Brooklyn, Williamsburg, &c.

PHILADELPHIA LINES.

			No.	Tonnage.
Boston	Line,	City of New York, Phineas Sprague and Kensington, (propellers,)	5	2,700
New York	"	Delaware, Boston, Kennebec, (sidewheels,)	3	2,100
Charleston	"	Keystone State, "	1	1,500
Savannah	"	The State of Georgia, "	1	1,500
Richmond	"	Virginia, Pennsylvania, City of Richmond, (propellers,)	3	1,350
			11	9,150

Two canal lines, The "Swift Sure," to New York, and the "Ericsson," to Baltimore.

FOREIGN AND DOMESTIC TONNAGE.

NEW YORK.	Tonnage cleared. American.	Foreign.	District. Registered.	Tonnage enrolled and Licensed.
1821 to 1830..	2,135,270	256,592	118,750	130,416
1831 to 1840..	4,346,975	2,672,623	130,932	169,906
1841 to 1850..	9,379,470	4,851,571	237,957	248,696
1851 to 1856..	11,036,018	6,431,282	518,575	522,439
PHILADELPHIA.				
1821 to 1830..	690,857	46,616	59,295	25,081
1831 to 1840..	571,286	136,989	51,293	29.226
1841 to 1850..	752,573	170,952	52,267	67,046
1851 to 1856..	641,038	258,020	69,425	214,948
The Yearly Average from 1821 to 1830.				
New York	213,527	25,659	11,875	13,041
Philadelphia..	69,085	4,661	5,929	2,508
From 1851 to 1856				
New York	1,839,336	1,071,880	86,428	87,073
Philadelphia..	106,839	4,303	11,381	35,824

THE INFLUENCE OF THE PENNSYLVANIA CENTRAL IN PROMOTING FOREIGN TRADE.

Two purposes were to be comprehended by the construction of this road—the development and accommodation of domestic trade, and the transportation of merchandise to and from the West. Doubtless, the first was a primary object, as its necessity was paramount and appealed to the interest of every citizen of the State ; but the other, though secondary, was not the less important, so far as foreign commerce was deemed one of the chief sources of prosperity. The geographical location of the

State, with reference to the West, North-west and South-west, gave her a position which could not be rivaled in any of the primary elements for attracting business. The capacity of the road for the dispatch of an almost unlimited trade, whether from within or without the State, was the result of a predetermined design to meet the future wants of both. In respect to the first object, there has been no failure; it has become the business vertebræ of the State, adding to her landed and mineral wealth, and fostering every branch of industry, which depends upon easy access to market for profit. But, in the second, it has not met with success commensurate with its capacity and advantages, or the expectations of its early projectors and patrons. An examination of the foreign shipments of breadstuffs and provisions, will not show an increase much beyond those made prior to its completion. In the item of flour alone, the returns of the road do not show a freightage equal to the surplus of State production. In other articles, peculiar to Western thrift, there is almost the same failure, to reach the point of just expectation. Upon the whole, it is entirely safe to assert that the road does not do the carrying trade of the State. In other words, if the entire surplus of State production could be concentrated upon this route, and the aggregate of State consumption of foreign goods be distributed by it, without accessions in respect to either, from without the State, its business would be much greater than it is at present. Hence, the road does not do the trade of a people equal in numbers to the population of the State. On the other hand, a simple calculation will show, that the canals and roads of New York do the carrying trade of fifteen to twenty millions of people; bringing their surplus of production, and taking back in return the various fabrics of foreign countries, and making the City of New York the focus of both.

Nor is it greatly in favor of the influence of the road upon foreign trade, to assert that our export trade is on the increase. Within the last ten years, the various domestic interests of the State have doubled, if not trebled, in the value of yearly returns. Necessarily this increase would first swell the coastwise and interior trade of the State, but a portion would also find its way into the official returns of exports. By allowing for this, and adding to it the official export returns, before the completion of the road, it will leave but a small sum by which to measure its influence in this respect.

Upon the import trade it has had a larger effect; yet not equal to the yearly advance of importation. The manufacturing industry of the State has had much to do with the progress of demand for foreign goods, not only by occasioning a greater importation of unprepared and raw materials, but also by enabling the community to pay for and consume a larger quantity of foreign goods than formerly.

The through freight on this road from Pittsburg in 1857, was about 94,909 tons; value, say, $5,000,000. All will admit, that its capacity is equal to ten times this amount, and that there is no lack of merchandise in the West seeking Eastern markets. Why, then, these comparatively insignificant results? Where rests the evil, and what the remedy for its removal, so that the enlargement of commerce in Philadelphia will follow upon the increased business of the road?

The Philadelphia Board of Trade, after great deliberation, have reported their conclusions upon this important subject. We will quote them:

" We believe Philadelphia may again be made to occupy her former proud position in the commercial world. . . . But how shall so desirable a result be accomplished? . . . Repeal the tonnage tax, and the real estate of Philadelphia, together with that within a belt of twenty miles on either side of the road, will very soon pay, upon its increased value, a revenue to the State equal to that derived from this tax. And we shall, moreover, preserve to our citizens a commerce which will constitute a continued source of prosperity and wealth. To procrastinate repeal would also be extremely unwise. Much advantage will be gained by attracting to the Pennsylvania road as large a proportion of trade as possible before the completion of the enlargement of the Erie canal shall enable it to carry at the low rates contemplated."

Here we have a simple and inexpensive remedy, to do away with a terrible incubus upon the trade of the road and the commerce of the city. It, most happily for Philadelphians, suggests the realization of large gains, without involving a dollar of expenditure. It would be a pleasing task, hereafter, to record the *unanimity of sentiment,* and the *harmonious exertion* that this prospect of not spending, nor risking anything to be sure of gaining much would occasion in the business classes of this city; but we dare not anticipate that task, since the report itself overturns this bucket-full of anticipations. In speaking of the energy and shrewdness of the New York merchants—the liberality of State legislation for commercial ends—the large banking capital, &c., they say,

"Hence, we find them extending to their merchants engaged in the important work of bringing the immense agricultural and other products of the interior to the seaboard, the monetary facilities which are necessary to fix their destination. With these they succeed in obtaining the hypothecation of the flour, wheat, bacon, hemp, &c., of the interior, to an unlimited extent, and no *railroad policy can divert it from its destination.**

Money has been advanced upon it in the West by New York merchants, and to that port it must go, although it may pass directly through our streets, and by our doors, in the cars of our own Pennsylvania Railroad Company, who have no power to control it or stop it on its way."

And again—

"It is conceded by all, that the amount of capital employed in the Western produce and transportation business is entirely inadequate to the necessities of the trade; at least, to that increase of it which we confidently predict must follow the repeal of the tonnage tax. To move the vast amount of Western produce which, under favorable circumstances, will find its natural outlet over our State improvement, will require a corresponding amount of active capital. This is not now in the hands of those engaged in this department of industry."

Thus, then, even while this tax *is in existence,* preventing the Pennsylvania Central road from doing a large Western trade (?) yet merchandise from the West passes directly through our streets, and by our doors, and whether this tax be repealed or not, the money of New York fixes the destination of the flour, wheat, bacon, hemp, &c., and "no railroad policy can divert it from its destination."

But they ruthlessly destroy all hope for harmonizing upon this grand remedy, this commercial panacea, when they add—

"We cannot refrain, however, from calling the attention of

* The italics are ours.

the Board to the fact that this *tax is paid exclusively* by the citizens of our own State; and mainly by the farmers, miners, and manufacturers located on the line of the road, the proceeds of whose industry find their way to market by this route. These must continue to pay it until it is removed. We know that a different impression is sought to be made in certain quarters, viz: that the *through or Western freight*, as well as the local, pays its proportion of the tax. But it is manifest that the competition between the several rival lines of communication for the Western tonnage, *does now and must always. prevent the Pennsylvania Railroad Company from obtaining rates upon it which will enable it to pay a tax to the State.* The consequence is, that, whilst the tonnage tax is ostensibly levied upon all tonnage passing over the road, the local freight owned by the citizens of Pennsylvania not only pays its own tax, but is forced to endure that which should be sustained by the freight from the West—thus reducing the value of the products of their industry to the extent of at least double the amount of the tax. There can be no greater or more mischievous mistake than to suppose that the Pennsylvania Railroad Company can contend successfully for the trade of the West, for any great length of time, with other rival lines, particularly those in the North, whilst burdened with a State tax. It may be that it will prove inadequate to the task, after being relieved of every unnecessary burden."

Shall the merchants of Philadelphia harmonize for relieving the trade of this road, when it now passes their doors notwithstanding the tax? *Facilitate the making of Philadelphia a way station for the " Pennsylvania Central and the Camden and Amboy Railroad ! !"* But even this is not all; it is conceded that any increase of business in Philadelphia would embarrass those engaged in the Western produce and transportation business. So, then, Philadelphia is to be doubly prevented from enjoying the benefits anticipated from the remedy advocated by the Board of Trade. And, absolutely, the Board recommends nothing to counteract the positive effects which must follow a repeal, if that repeal would result as they most hopefully predict. We are happy, however, in being able to say, that they deny the efficacy of their own remedy, when they are constrained to observe that this tax is paid exclusively by the citizens of our own State. Had they not thus positively denied that the Western trade was, in the least degree, prevented from seeking this road for the East, we should have reasoned back from effect to cause, and insisted, for the salvation of the business interests of Philadelphia, upon *preventing* the abolition of this tax—to hold on to it until we were prepared to control the increased trade, both, by adopting the plan of the New York merchants, and having Western goods hypothecated, and their destination directed, to Philadelphia, and by being prepared to do the business with convenience and profit. We would have recommended this course, in order to prevent the result so truthfully predicted upon the want of those requisite facilities for terminating the increase of business in this City, viz:

" Trade, when once directed in a given channel, cannot be diverted therefrom without extraordinary effort. Hence the importance of securing our share without delay, and the propriety of removing, at once, every obstacle in the way of its speedy accomplishment."

The obliquity of commercial foresight, so plainly apparent throughout this document, is only excusable on the plea, that with some men it is deemed more dignified to be obstinately wrong than to yield their influence to a scheme not originating with themselves.

The conclusions of the following paragraphs will convince every person, that the Board of Trade should hereafter confine their reports to figures, and eschew all arguments on commercial matters:

" The conclusion at which your Committee have arrived, and to which they wish most particularly to call the attention of the Board of Trade, and their fellow-citizens generally, is that, *as we succeed in bringing to our city the produce of the South and West, we shall increase our commercial and general prosperity.* It is at this point that we must begin the work.

We need not now concern ourselves about steam lines or packet ships. Let us crowd our warehouses with the bacon, hemp, flour, and cotton of the South and West, and we shall soon see approaching our wharves the ships necessary to carry it to foreign markets, and these, ladened with rich cargoes of merchandise for domestic consumption and Western distribution, will give active business to our merchants, and profitable freights to our railroad companies in transporting them to their destination.

We would not, however, be understood as undervaluing the

importance of steam or other communication with foreign countries. The establishment of steam lines and packet ships to
convey abroad the produce which we hope to attract, by the
liberal policy we suggest, from the West to our ports, is indispensable, and, if possible, the movements should be simulta-
neously made. The early establishment of such lines would
save much temporary inconvenience; but, in the opinion of
your Committee, the *primary* and *leading* object should be
to secure the Western trade. This accomplished, foreign
commerce, being the legitimate outgrowth of domestic trade,
will speedily adapt itself to our necessities."

They at once throw aside the most important adjunct to
modern commercial progress, ignore its efficacy in building up
trade, and urge the bringing of Western produce to our city,
without showing, in the remotest degree, the cause for its not
coming now, or upon what inducements more will come in the
future, than at present. Let us crowd our warehouses with the
bacon, hemp, flour and cotton of the South and West! Does
the tax prevent you from doing this now? No, you have said
that the tax was paid *exclusively* by our own people. If you
need not concern yourselves about steam lines or packet ships,
you ought then to find it easy to crowd your warehouses, and
still more easy to keep them crowded. Since, according to your
view, excepting the want of business foresight, there is nothing to
prevent the one, and, most certainly, no means of relief in the other.
It is true, that you acknowledge some temporary inconvenience
would be saved by establishing a line of steam vessels, simulta-
neously, with crowding your warehouses, but, if not possible,
it is no cause for worryment, since it would be quite impossible
for a *temporary* inconvenience to continue. Why? Simply
because the West would not be deluded into crowding you a
second time. It is quite as plain, that the "primary and leading
object" has been all along, to "secure the Western trade," as
it is *now* untrue that foreign commerce is the legitimate outgrowth of domestic trade, and that it will speedily adapt itself
to our necessities. It can be asserted, without fear of contradiction, that foreign trade will concentrate at no port, no matter
what may be the inland facilities for concentrating the products
of the soil, unless by the employment of capital in the best
modern means for ocean transportation. This is especially true,

7

when two ports are closely contiguous, one of which has both facilities, and the other only one. Ocean steam-vessels are only the embodiment of that capital which will seek only those points where it will be sure of profitable returns. Hence no outside capital will undertake to adapt itself to our necessities, that is, to the building up of our foreign commerce. If you cannot convince resident capital of the profit that is to ensue upon the crowding of your warehouses, you will not be able to convince non-resident capital. At the port of New Orleans, a large export trade is done, nearly equal to that at New York, yet a very small import trade. The reason is obvious. There is no other outlet for the peculiar staples composing that trade, and the nature of the trade is such that it is sufficiently profitable to allow vessels engaged in it, to return in ballast, or loaded for other ports. Such can never be the case in Philadelphia.

Western goods find an outlet at New York, and reach that point on terms quite as good as they can reach Philadelphia. After this fact is established capital controls the balance, and those goods will naturally find the port at which capital is most advantageously employed to take them hence. If sailing vessels are still to be resorted to, for doing the increased business, to follow upon crowded warehouses, they will be found utterly incompetent for the task of competition, and no line of steamers will be seen to approach our wharves to relieve us of the temporary inconvenience, until they are convinced that the import trade will furnish return cargoes.

The Board of Trade seem to be insensible to the fact, that a city acquires a reputation for doing a certain kind of business, precisely in the same way as a firm of private individuals, and that neither will attract that for which they are wholly unprepared, and have the reputation of not doing. It is well known in the West, that Philadelphia has not the means, and is wholly devoid of the reputation of doing a foreign trade. Is it, then, reasonable to suppose, that Western merchants, having the choice of routes, will prefer to employ an agent wholly unprepared to transact his business, to one who has been doing it, and is able to continue to do it on more advantageous terms? After all, these men of the West decide where their produce shall go, and New York, like a mercantile house of great reputation for means and dispatch of business, will be preferred to any other house of less means and pretensions.

Here, then, is "the point at which to begin." Enlarge your means for the transaction of business—get up a reputation of being able to do business on the most advantageous terms, by the use of capital in those facilities which are essential to success, and then take off restrictions, if any exist, and invite trade. Concern yourselves about steam vessels—enlarge your market —then go out West and solicit business—then circulate Philadelphia newspapers, brag and bluster a little, and your road will do a largely increasing business, and Philadelphia may again be made to occupy her former proud position in the commercial world.

From what has been said, it must be apparent that the tonnage tax is not the evil, and its repeal is not the remedy required to improve the business of the Pennsylvania Central road, with the view of promoting foreign trade at this port. It is in that view alone that we have alluded to the report of the Board of Trade, and not because we thought the tax just, politic or proper, as a source of State revenue ; and while, therefore, in the abstract, we do not oppose the wishes of the Board, we deem it, under the circumstance, a commercial blunder for Philadelphia merchants to advocate its immediate, unconditional repeal. They are not prepared to take advantage of the expected result; while they might secure inestimable advantages by making its further existence subservient to commercial ends.

A just comprehension of their own interests, in combination with that of the City and State, should also induce the railroad company to seek no other than a conditional repeal. The greatest scope for the profitable working of the road, lies in the increased commercial prosperity of Philadelphia. Let them seek to make her a depot for the products of the West, by facilitating the direct importation of goods, and their business will quadruple in five years.

But this Company see their interests differently. They urge an immediate and unconditional repeal ; and, if unsuccessful, will appeal to the Courts for redress. In the latter case, we do not see what is to prevent a successful issue, at least to the amount of tax for which the through trade is responsible. Being relieved of this, they well know that no hesitation will be made in any legislature as to the removal of the tax from the local freight.

We have neither the right nor the disposition to censure this Company for using all proper means to release themselves from an onerous tax. Nor would we allude to this in any way, were it not to show, that all their movements are predicated upon the fact, that they can no longer rely upon the sagacity nor the enterprise of the merchants of Philadelphia. The Board of Trade, while being used to advocate what would result in no benefit to the City, has unwittingly damned, with faint support, what was most essential. Hence, to take care of themselves, becomes a matter of paramount necessity. They drive the starting wedge by the repeal, and they follow it up by preparing the means of extending their business independent of Philadelphia and her commerce.

We commend the following resolution, now published for the information of the stockholders, to the attention of our mercantile readers :

" *Resolved*, That the Board of Directors of the Pennsylvania Railroad Company be, and they are hereby, authorised to select the most eligible location on the Delaware river for a terminal depot, to be reached by locomotive steam-power, and to cause the extension of the road to the said river, to be completed at the earliest practicable period.

By order of the Board.

J. EDGAR THOMSON, *President.*"

The report to which this resolution is appended, contains the inducements for thus extending the road, and from it we transfer the following paragraphs :

" A merchant receiving flour at both New York and Philadelphia, from the same Western consignor, and selling it at precisely the same rate in each city, returns to the consignor a larger per centage on his Philadelphia than on his New York sales—arising solely from the cost of transportation in favor of Philadelphia ; consequently cheap transportation to the river front secures to her a large trade which otherwise she cannot obtain, and no doubt vessels will be brought here for the trade thus created. This advantage will not be left unimproved by those controlling the commercial interests of our city.

In conclusion, your Board of Directors are of the opinion that the Pennsylvania Railroad has not accomplished the object of its construction until a connection is effected with tide-water on the Delaware, thus opening an avenue by which every variety of mineral and agricultural production can be conveyed to a proper point for shipment, and furnishing facilities for the trade of this city at least equal to those of any location on the Atlantic coast."

Without stopping to notice the above positive contradiction of the whole tone, and some of the statements of the Board of Trade Report, we have to remark that the railroad company are fully aware that there are none who "control the commercial interests of our city," ready to improve the advantages thus proffered—they are consequently aware that the "vessels brought here for the trade thus created," will have to be brought by themselves. And as to giving a "new impetus to the growth of Philadelphia," "tending more to revive our commerce than any other measure," and causing "flouring mills to be erected," and the packing of pork to be carried on, in the vicinity of this "shipping point," (all of which are mentioned in the report,) they are blinds, not intended to be so, but nevertheless, blinds for those who control the commercial interests of our city. They have waited sufficiently long for the business men of the city to adopt the only means calculated to "revive commerce," and they are determined to promote the interests of the road by other means. This is most clearly intimated in the second paragraph quoted, when the Board of Directors truthfully remark, "that the Pennsylvania Railroad has not accomplished the object of its construction until a connection is made with the waters of the Delaware," which simply means that its capacity for business has not been equalled by the establishing of corresponding facilities for foreign trade. The Company are, therefore, forced to employ this method, so that "every variety of mineral and agricultural production can be *conveyed to a proper point of shipment.*"

Whilst we need *not now* concern ourselves about steam-ship or packets, the Company will, in their absence, own or procure the proper vessels to convey freight by the Delaware to the proper point for shipment, N. York; since no man will be so stupid as to believe that sailing craft will be used for exporting purposes, or that the simple fact of completing this extension will establish a line of ocean steamships. Hence, two consequences must irresistably follow; Philadelphia will wholly loose her foreign trade—(it will then be too late to attempt to obtain home capital to build up a line of steam-vessels,) and the Philadelphia public will impotently struggle against a destiny which might have been prevented; doubtless, City Councils will be convened, the Board of Trade will report, some newspapers will be enraged, some will remain unruffled, others will laugh, while those of New York will join in the *laughing* chorus.

Enough has been said to show, that the influence of the Pennsylvania Central Railroad, for the promotion of foreign trade, has been but limited, and that the only policy advocated by the Board of Trade, would prove as ineffective as the arguments of their report are forced, fallacious and contradictory. And, in anticipation of success in their projects by the Rail-road Company, may we hope that sufficient has been said to arouse the thinking, reasoning men of Philadelphia, to the necessity of adopting enlarged views of Commercial policy, in order to prevent being over-reached, on the one hand, by the failure of temporizing expedients, and on the other, by the unresisted sway of corporate enterprise, acting independently of their substantial interests, and excluding for the future, the only legitimate means for the promotion of foreign commerce, viz;—Trans-Atlantic Steamship Communication.

STEAM UPON THE OCEAN AS ESSENTIAL TO COMMERCE AS STEAM UPON LAND.

The railroad and steam car is one of the exponents of progress and civilization. The necessities of a growing and expanded country demanded their introduction as the most speedy means of intercommunication and interchange of commodities. The introduction of steam upon the ocean was the result of the same laws of progress, and is now as absolutely essential to commerce as steam upon land. Take the locomotive from the Erie and Central Railroads of New York, and prevent the steam navigation of the Erie canal, and grass would grow in Broad-

way in less than a twelvemonth. Or remove from her harbor
the thirty-seven ocean steamers which now place her in constant and speedy communication with every important port on
the Eastern and Western coast of the Atlantic, and you will
produce nearly the same result. Her early success in securing
the best means of reaching the West was followed by the best
means of reaching Europe. The one acted as a counterpoise to
the other, and unitedly have accomplished what one could not
have done in the absence of the other. Whilst she was building railroads to maintain a commercial monopoly on land, she
was building steamboats to secure the same on sea, and she
has been successful in both.

The introduction of Steamboats was very gradual, and many
years passed after their use upon interior waters, before they
were employed on the Ocean. The first practically used in the
World, was the North River, built by Fulton, at New York,
1807. The first Steamboat which crossed the Atlantic, was
also built in the same City, in 1819. In 1840 the entire steamboat tonnage of the United States was about 160,000 tons; in
England, in 1836, only 68,000 tons. In April, 1838, the Steam-
ship Sirius and the Great Western arrived in New York, one
from Cork and the other from Bristol. Following soon after,
came the British Queen, then the Cunard Liverpool, Halifax and
Boston line. Since then, the use of Steam upon the Ocean for
commercial purposes has become general, and no doubt is entertained of its eventually, and at an early day, superceding sailing
vessels, wherever foreign commerce is at all important. There
is the same necessity for speed and certainty in the communication between commercial nations, as between contiguous states,
and the decline of commerce is inevitable wherever the agency
of steam is not, or cannot be established: especially must this
be true of a Port which, by vicinity of location, is forced into
a competition with another, possessed of this essential agent,
in connection with every advantage of interior transportation.
With one exception, the Port of Philadelphia has never had the
benefit of this great revolutionizer of Commerce upon the Ocean,
and her present Commercial Status affords sufficient evidence
of the necessity of a speedy reformation in this respect.

In another place we have alluded to the reasons which operated against the energetic pursuit of commerce in Philadelphia. They need not be repeated here to show that the absence of steam vessels was one of the most direct consequences. In addition, however, to the fact that commercial enterprise was exhausted by interior investments, it may be stated here that until within the last eight or ten years, there was much to discourage the establishment of such facilities for trade. The State works had failed originally, and, although yearly increasing in amount of business, mismanagement continued to prevent them from earning sufficient to clear expenses. In the meantime, the progress made by New York, overshadowed and over awed lesser communities. The Briarean arms of her enterprise, reached to almost every part of the Union, grasping and using with a giants power, every facility to accelerate her own interests, heedless, and designedly so, of all opposition. The principal of centralization has been, and continues to be, the life and soul of her policy. The influence of her capital penetrated everywhere. States as well as Cities came within the purview of her grand scheme of consolidation; the one cajoled into granting franchises detrimental to local enterprise, and destructive of independent action; the other forced into a tributary alliance, by the cordon of iron highways, the management of which she now controls by her antecedent prestige, and out-reaching business instinct. In fact, she has become the commercial bully of America.

Co-operating with this quasi mental intimidation, which prevented capitalists from encountering that predjudice which effectuates a prejudged failure, was the fact that manufacturing, and the quieter pursuits of money getting, "by cent per cent," had contracted and individualised the enterprise of our community. The magnates in commerce of fifty years ago were gone, and few were present born to commerce, and fewer, those who were reared in its liberalizing atmosphere. That dashing recklessness and those expansive views, which challenge success, and spring from the handling of millions in daily business, were not the characteristics of the Philadelphia Merchant, from the mere laws of education and habit.

There is, then, no cause for surprise in this fact, that Philadelphia has not been supplied with the modern improvements in ocean transport. Nor is it a matter of wonder, that even at the present time, there are many doubts, much hesitation, great timidity and a wide spread division of sentiment, upoh this subject.

But the time has arrived when further delay grows pregnant with danger; doubt and hesitation must give way to alarm, and timidity be changed to energetic action;—the establishment of a line of Ocean Steam Vessels is the one-great-absorbing-over-ruling-necessity, and, in the language of the Board of Trade, used, however, for another object, "it can be effected only by the most cordial and energetic co-operation of all classes of citizens. All groundless jealousies must be suppressed ﾠin a patriotic resolution to promote the Commerce and Industry of the City and State."

THE COMMISSION AND IMPORTING MERCHANTS.

In order to prove that our conclusions are correct, we will appeal to the business of the Commission and Importing Merchants of Philadelphia.

The former has three markets in which to dispose of his consignments; the home, those of neighbouring states, or that created by foreign shipment. The first is necessarily confined to consumption; hence, so soon as the supply exceeds the home demand, one of the others must reduce the surplus to save consignors from the effects of reduced prices. Should there be no foreign demand, the merchant suffers or is compelled to seek relief by forwarding a portion of his stock to a domestic market from whence it can be shipped. This resort is always hazardous. It establishes a sub-agency by which the owner and the merchant is deprived of that supervision, expected in the one case and necessary in the other. If the stuff is consigned to New York, it must submit to immediate sale, at ruling rates. Two commissions must be charged, or the merchant wholly looses his, if the price at which sale is effected, is fully accounted for to his owner. In addition to this the incidental charges of this

8

consignment are more than doubled, so that the speculation is an exceedingly fortunate one, if all can be borne by the increase of price in New York, over that obtainable in Philadelphia. In the majority of instances this is impossible; and the consequence is, that in the absence of a foreign demand, advices must be sent West, that the market of Philadelphia is *overstocked, prices have declined, hold back your shipments.* To the Western shipper this is a chronic complaint, and is conclusive against the capacity of the Philadelphia market, he therefore divides his consignments, or concludes to send entirely to New York, where sale is always certain. Hence, it becomes almost folly for the forwarding merchant to solicit trade from the West; he cannot stand under a pressure of stock, if successful, unless his capital is enormous; and if it is, he has no sort of guarantee, that commissions, storage, interest and the payment of freight bills and drafts, will not leave the shipper in his debt.

Were it possible to create a foreign demand in this market, all difficulty would disappear. The price current would not indicate that anomalous fluctuation which is occasioned by receipts instead of demands. In almost every other commercial market, demand is the barometer of price; but in Philadelphia, the *dough-trough* is king "on change," and buys largely only when a full market allows him to dictate the terms, and never buys beyond immediate wants, when the supply keeps even pace with demand. As to foreign shipments, the rule is also reversed, they are seldom made, because prices rule high in Europe, but because a depressed home market permits the merchant to make speculative cargoes, bought at prices which can stand the hazard of a shut-eye venture. Indeed, no prudent man would attempt to buy regularly for foreign consumption in this market unless upon his own terms, since he must either charter a vessel himself and freight her, or wait the advertisement of a "chance for Liverpool." In the latter case, he is unable to draw upon his separate purchases and must stand the loss of interest or the benefit of rapid re-investments. Many months have elapsed since a vessel has been "put up" for any foreign port, and even the old line of Packets have had to go south for cargo. There is scarcely a foreign or even a domestic house now located in Philadelphia, exclusively engaged in the purchase of breadstuff for European markets, and no foreign capital except when a speculation in this market draws it from New York.

The commission merchant is, then, by necessity, confined to the demands of home consumption and the coastwise trade, both of which can be, and are so managed, that a large stock is purchased upon a depressed market, and a hand to hand stock upon a rising one. In self-defence, and by common consent, consignments from the West must be limited to that kind of demand, and to do business at all, he must peddle flour by the barrel and sell wheat " by the small."

The importing merchant has difficulties of another character, but more easily remedied. Since exports and imports bear the corresponding relation of outward and homeward cargo, it becomes a fixed law of trade, that the same character of vessels employed in the one, must be employed in the other, or return in ballast, or what is quite as bad for the port of departure, return with freight for another market. If, therefore, sailing vessels are exclusively used in the Foreign Trade, the importer must be confined to the facilities offered by them, or he must resort to those offered by the most convenient port. This has already taken place in Philadelphia to an alarming extent. We have stated that the importation via New York on Philadelphia account, amounted in 1857, to Six Millions. This value must annually increase since the tendency of importation is to concentrate at one point where the greatest facilities can be obtained at fixed periods, and in the speediest manner. The reason is obvious; by far the largest value of foreign goods is for ornament, luxury and fashion; all of these are constantly changing, requiring the importer to renew his stock frequently and keep pace with the reported change of mode, by constantly opening new goods. Sailing vessels cannot fulfil these demands. The fashions of Paris and London, and the fabrics of Europe can appear on Broadway in twenty days; they must be on Chestnut St. in the same time; in other words, Levy in Philadelphia must have the same facilities as Stewart in New York.

This tendency to concentration, having diverted fully one-third of the whole import trade from this City, has a reactive effect against the purchase and shipment of export cargoes. A homeward freight is thus, yearly, becoming more uncertain.

The equilibrium having been destroyed, there remains but little inducement to put up vessels here for foreign ports. Indeed, the foreign trade of the City is chiefly owing to the liberality and pluck of the proprietors of the Cope Line of Packets, and the determination of many Market Street Firms to import for the Fall and Spring trade by home lines. But it is fast becoming evident, that the periodical nature of that trade will not support vessels required to make round trips throughout the year. If a homeward cargo was always certain, breadstuffs could be taken from here, even when the price in foreign markets would not justify shipments; the loss of freight being preferable to going in ballast, or breaking the continuity of regular trips. However beneficial this would be to the breadstuff market, no line of vessels can be maintained by profitless outward and only periodical homeward cargoes. Hence it is, as we have remarked, that no vessels have been put up for foreign ports for months, and this line has been compelled to seek business in the Southern Trade.

These facts are all so self-evident that argument is superfluous. The commission merchant wants, and must have, the demand of a foreign market, and the importer would use exclusively, that home line, which affords this to the former, and unitedly, a profitable business must be the result.

WILL A PHILADELPHIA LINE OF OCEAN STEAMSHIPS PAY?

A brief reference to the old Philadelphia and Liverpool line will afford some data in this respect.

This line of vessels was not originated by Philadelphians; it was owned and controlled by foreign capitalists, who appreciated the capacity of the city for trade, and believed that a profitable business could be done, by affording a means of outlet to the agricultural productions of the interior and those of the West, brought to her market. It was also calculated, that the importation of goods, direct to Philadelphia, would be greatly increased by affording those accommodations which were sought in a neighboring port. They based the success of their enterprise upon a simple law of trade, viz: that capital must find profit in facilitating the exchange of foreign merchandise for domestic commodities, at a port where the one is largely demanded, and the surplus of the other finds a natural depot; and where the supply of the one, and demand for the other, must keep pace with the progress of production and consumption.

The first boat of this line, " The City of Glasgow," commenced running in 1850 ; she was followed by " The City of Manchester," in 1852, and " The City of Philadelphia," in 1854. In the meanwhile two other boats were built, viz: " The City of Washington" and "The City of Baltimore ;" and the Kangaroo purchased for the purpose of adding to the efficiency of the line. The two boats last mentioned were never regularly engaged in this trade. "The City of Glasgow" and "The City of Philadelphia" were lost, the former being entirely paid for by her earnings. "The City of Manchester," in eighteen months, had earned more than half her cost in the same trade, after which she, with the others,were used for transports in the Crimea.

This withdrawal of these boats, from their legitimate trade, has been used as an argument in proof of the unprofitable result of the enterprise. Five facts contradict this conclusion, two of which have already been stated. The third fact is, that two years after the first, the second boat was added; in about the same time the third, and then two were built and one bought, *all* for the same line. Obstinacy may be a characteristic with both the English and Scotch, but they are not often known to be obstinately losing money in an undertaking which may be dropped, or changed in direction, at any moment, and which certainly need not be renewed after being suspended : this makes our fourth fact consist in the endeavour of the Company to re-establish their business relations with Philadelphia, with four boats after their return. The fifth arises out of the well known demand and high prices paid by the English government, during the Russian war, for steam transports. The prices offered in cash, for the use of such vessels, were sufficient to tempt any Company, throwing aside the promptings of patriotism, to desist temporarily from the prosecution of a trade which could again be resumed. In confirmation of this, it may be added, that in reference to " The City of Manchester," an incident occurred which proves that the trade as well as the

Crimean service, were profitable; a Quaker Lady, opposed to war, had an interest in this boat, for which she was paid entire, with an immense bonus, $70,000, after fully one-half her interest had been paid to her from the earnings.

It was perfectly just and natural that difficulty would be experienced in rebuilding a trade, unceremoniously given up, causing loss, disappointment and derangement in the business of all its patrons. Confidence once lost, is not readily restored, especially in business matters, of which it is the soul. It was, as it always is, far easier to build up, than to rebuild. The Company had patience for the first, but not for the last, and they became discouraged.

But there ought to be no necessity to appeal to the past, to prove that a line of Steamers will pay now and hereafter. It is a commercial necessity—not for the trade now done in Philadelphia, but for that which can be done—not for the bread-Stuffs which now reach our Store-houses—but that which can be brought here—not for the foreign goods now sold in Philadelphia—but what can be distributed West, Northwest, South, and Southwest. If there is a business man who can carry his eye along the magnificent avenues of trade, penetrating to all these most distant points, and making as it were a fan, the handle of which lies in the grasp of Philadelphia, and does not see the trade which can, and ought to be, winnowed, as it were, into the garners of Broad and Front street, he is either stricken with the palsy or provincialism.

But let us briefly specify some of the sources of business which must concur in making a properly organized line profitable.

1st. It is absolutely essential to the grain or breadstuff market. The commission men are constantly burthened with a stock for which there is no outlet. There is no stability nor buoyancy in the market, and neither can be enjoyed until regular, speedy and fixed periods of shipment afford facilities to take advantage of prices abroad. Establish these facilities and everything favors the termination of Western consignments in Philadelphia to an unlimited amount. We may add, that the Philadelphia and Liverpool line did a large and paying business in shipping flour and grain; the resident agent making regular purchases on account of his owners, and sufficient was freighted for others to make up a full cargo.

2d. The import trade must follow the export, so soon as the proper facilities are supplied, and the growth of the one will be as constant as that of the other. From twenty to thirty millions of goods are now distributed from this point ; that amount will be doubled in five years, if the city is made, even, an important depot for exportation.

3d. The City of New York will use the Philadelphia line to a certain extent simply, because goods can be passed through the Custom House here so much more speedily than in that city. Pittsburg, Cincinnati, St. Louis and Baltimore will use this line ; all of which import more or less, with the disposition to increase, if the proper facilities were afforded. In this respect, Philadel-phia would give them advantages unattainable in New York. The merchants of Baltimore used the former line to a great extent, and would find it to their interest to import by a new one when properly established.

4th. The emigrant travel to and from Europe could be controlled by such a line, greatly to its profit, and the convenience of those people. The lines of rail from the west would most naturally and cheaply concentrate them here, if they had cheap, safe and moderately speedy means of transit hence. The Philadel-phia and Liverpool line did a large and emigrant passenger business, not so much from the fact that it was a feature in the management of the line, but more from the fact that New York is the horror of an emigrant arrived or arriving.

5th. Foreign capital would immediately find inducement sufficient to bring it to this city. European connections would be established, the reputation of our city enhanced, and the business integrity and high character of our merchants appreciated both at home and abroad. These would be no slight advantages in growing business for such a line.

6th. By stimulating commerce it would lay the foundation for almost unlimited success. The apathy and languor which so often affects trade would give place to activity and enterprise.' Business men would be kept in perpetual occupation, their minds would acquire new vigor, become enlarged in powers and facili-ties, and more comprehensive in the conception and execution of commercial operations. These influences would be felt in every branch of the mechanical and fine arts, opening a larger field for invention, and stimulating every department and division of labor. Nor would these effects be confined to the city—the interior would feel the same impulses and be affected with the same spirit of reaction and enlargement.

OBJECTORS AND OBJECTIONS.

It would be unprecedented in the annals of Philadelphia, to be hereafter noted by another Watson, amiably curious in reviving sweet reminiscences, if this undertaking did not find *objectors* and meet with *objections*. Every step of progress has been contested, every departure from established usage reprobated, and every advocate of improvement has been crushed by the heavy logic of illogical stability. As a mere illustration, we might mention the heavy logic of a protest against lighting this great City with gas, the protestants preferring the ancient and unctuous substance called oil, or penny-dips. Among the *appalling* consequences urged, was the apprehended destruction of "shad and herring" in the Delaware. The passenger railroad discussion will in time afford some choice relics, and the protestants against the removal of the market houses, forsooth, on account of their "*ancient* and fish-like smell," must have their memory preserved in the " curious chronicles of Philadelphia."

In the commencement of an enterprise, new, and of an important public nature, objectors and objections must be expected, as the boy in the commencement of his life must expect the mumps and the measles, because every other boy has had them. But neither one nor the other ought to be feared, while both must be tolerated.

There can be no objection urged against establishing a line of Steamers, to ply between Philadelphia and foreign ports, that cannot be overcome by proper management and well directed energy. It is a favorite argument with some, that the Collins Line at New York was not sustained, and *ergo*, no line can be maintained at Philadelphia. A very little reflection should convince every one, that the reasonable profits of years of successful trade were sunk in the extravagant tinsel ornament and furniture of those vessels. Their cost was nearly, if not quite treble, what it should have been ; and the disbursements to maintain a correspondence in the etiquet of their management, would be sufficient to discharge the entire expenses of a business line at this port.

The trade of Philadelphia does not require such boats, and no matter how cheaply they can be purchased, they would *provoke* a failure of the whole undertaking. On the contrary, the plainest and most substantially, as well as newly built propellers, with a tonnage ranging from 1500 to 2000, and costing not under one hundred, and not exceeding one hundred and twenty-five dollars to the ton of tonnage measurement,—and not exceeding three, built so as to afford comfortable quarters for 2d and 3d class passengers, with very limited cabin accommodations, and large storage, would comprehend the wants of trade, and prove a highly profitable investment.

Another objection of a physical character is made, viz: that the navigation of the Delaware is subject to interruption by ice, and there is no effective means used to keep the channel open. In the first place, this obstruction, like all of its class, will give way to interest and enterprise. Interest a sufficient number of men in shipping, in ship chandlery, in rigging, stevedore work and the thousand employments made to flourish by an export and import trade, and there will be no necessity for an appeal to City Councils to furnish and maintain ice boats There will be plenty of them, and they *will do the work*.

But all fear of injury from this cause can be removed by preparing accommodations at New Castle, to be used in case of any accidental detention by the fixedness of the ice. From this place there is frequent and cheap communication with this city, and no large expense would be incurred by the management, or fall upon freighters, if one or two of the line is compelled, during a temporary obstruction, to arrive and depart at this point.

But even this difficulty is magnified beyond truth or reason, as will be seen in a record of climate, made up from Hazard's Register, and embracing eleven winters, from 1818 to the winter of 1829.

9

1818, Jan. 31. River closed. Feb. 28. The ice gave way. Dec. River obstructed.

1819, Jan. 4. Arrivals—not wholly closed again during the Winter. Dec. clear all month.

1820, Jan. 1. Ice at Reedy Island; closed from the 4th to the 20th. 27th Ice again. Feb. 4. Bay full of ice, 16 arrivals. Dec. clear all the month.

1821, Jan. 4. Much ice in the Bay. Feb. 14. closed since 12th Jan. Dec. River free.

1822, Jan. 8. Ice, but not closed. No mention of ice in Feb. Dec. Arrivals.

1823, Jan. 22. Navigation not obstructed. Feb. No remark. Dec. arrivals.

1824, Jan. No mention of ice. Feb. do. Dec. Arrivals.

1825. Jan. No mention of ice. Feb. 14. "A May day." Dec. 28, several vessels in the ice.

1826, Jan. River free from ice; 31, closed. Feb. 3, skating; 8, open. Dec. Arrivals.

1827, Jan. No mention of ice. Feb. do. Dec. No obstruction.

1828, During the whole winter navigation uninterrupted. Dec. 27, Thus far has remained open.

These records were kept with the view of noting the "effects of climate upon navigation;" and, therefore, whenever the river was frozen, so as to offer any obstruction, mention was made of it. Of the 33 winter months, during those years, it will be found that only thirteen affected navigation, whilst no mention is made of ice in the other twenty; and in only one winter the fixedness of the ice continued for thirty days. In nearly all of the others the obstruction lasted but a few days. Possibly, in the whole period of ten years, there would not have been a detention of sixty days to the periodical arrival and departure of boats, or the average of six days to the year. When we consider that the winters of thirty years ago, were greatly more severe than the winters of late years, there does not seem to be much reason to fear that this difficulty will be insurmountable.

The channel of the Delaware, it is well known, is nowhere less than 4 fathoms in depth, excepting below Fort Mifflin, where, for a short distance, at extremely low tide, it is a few feet less.

CONCLUSION.

In the course of these pages, we have shown, that the early rivalry in commerce, resulted in favor of New York, by reason of her superior physical advantages for inland trade, over those of Philadelphia. That the enterprise and capital of her citizens were first turned to the construction of artificial channels, to meet the wants of the future empire growth of the West—by which, again, she took precedence of Philadelphia, and maintained it without any material competition from the State works of Pennsylvania. When the construction of railroads made competition possible, she again took the initiative by the building of railways, especially adapted to accommodation of the travel and trade from the West, North-west and South-west, to interfere with which there was no like improvement in Pennsylvania until 1853. Then, in order to account for this delay in making up the defects of the canal by the construction of a trunk line of railway, to the western border of the State, we have shown that the mines of the State, and the necessity of immense improvements to utilize their products, absorbed both the capital and mind of the mercantile classes in Philadelphia. We have followed this up by showing what has been done for the development of State wealth, making a sum of interior resource possibly unequalled by a like area of territory in the world, containing the same amount of population; making the conclusion almost self-evident that commerce could not have been a successful cotemporaneous pursuit. After thus showing that the "manifest destiny" of the State was based upon indestructable foundations, having every interior element, whether in mineral productions, in agricultural wealth, in roads and canals, or in manufacturing establishments, for the greatest maximum of success, we developed the fact, that she is now enabled to compete, *so far as inland transportation was concerned*, for the trade of the West, North-west, South and South-west, upon equal, if not superior terms, with any and all States further North.

We then attempted to place before the reader a figure calculation and tables, in order to show what a portion of this trade has already yielded, upon which he may imagine its future growth, and the rich rewards of those Eastern cities, able to share in its transportation and distribution. Impressed with its present immensity and its future magnificence, we then proceeded to show, that up to this time Philadelphia was still excluded from any great participation in its profits, and was not possessed of those exterior steam facilities indispensable to their acquisition in the future. The business and wants of the commission and importing merchant gave cumulative proof, not alone of the want, but also of the necessity of such accommodations. We then asserted that a line of ocean steamships would do a profitable business now, and increase their profits out of the prosperity they would of themselves accelerate. In order to place this beyond all cavil or distrust, we instanced the success of a line commenced under comparatively unfavorable auspices, and enforced our opinion by citing some of the causes which must minister to the business and bring profit to a new enterprise.

The scope of the subject, and the manner adopted to arrive at the conclusions we wished to enforce, required the introduction of statistical tables, with other like matter, and we have done so, much beyond what was necessary for immediate illustration, but they were deemed valuable and not at all injurious to the matter or the reader. For the imperfections and shortcomings found in the course of the work, we make no apology, lest our politeness prevents some other person from doing the same thing in a better way. We might have discussed other topics of corelative interests, and it was our intention so to do, but this pamphlet is a pioneer, in its way, and may already be too long. In place of that, however, we might mention, that a pamphlet has been distributed, to some extent, among the business men of Philadelphia, prepared under the same auspices, and directed to the same end; but in the shape of a proposition to make the conditional repeal of the "Tonnage Tax," now levied on the business of the Pennsylvania Central, a means for furnishing a fixed capital of $1,000,000—and $500,000 to be added from private subscriptions, with which to establish a line of steamships upon a sure basis. To that, the reader who has reached this page, is most respectfully referred.

We will here end as we began, by repeating, that a point has been reached in the commercial history of Philadelphia, from which further progress is impossible, and recession inevitable, unless those facilities, indispensable to the successful pursuit to commerce, are speedily and permanently established.